MORNA'S MAGIC & MISTLETOE - A NOVELLA

BOOK 8.5 OF MORNA'S LEGACY SERIES

BETHANY CLAIRE

Editor: Dj Hendrickson
Cover Designed by Damonza

Available In eBook, Paperback, & Hardback

eBook ISBN: 978-1-947731-50-9
Paperback ISBN: 978-1-947731-51-6
Hardback ISBN: 978-1-947731-52-3

http.//www.bethanyclaire.com

For Mom,

Because Christmas stories are your favorites.

CHAPTER 1

cMillan Castle, Scotland—December of 1651

itsy is watching me again. She isn't normally awake so early, but with Baodan away for a fortnight to assist our friends at Cagair Castle, she's allowed young Rodric to sleep in her bed, and the child kicks in his sleep like an angry mule. For the past three nights she's slipped out of her bed the moment her son fell asleep and retreated to his bed. Rodric believes he's getting the special treat of snuggling with his mother while his father is away, but both of them end up getting a good night's sleep. Unlike many of my other grandchildren, I'm not certain a flock of geese flying straight through Rodric's bedchamber would wake him. Come morning, the wee babe is none the wiser to his mother's trickery.

The only complication comes in when I wake up at my usual time each morning. My bedchamber sits right next to Rodric's and as is normal for all mothers of young children, the slightest unexpected noise wakes Mitsy. Try as I might to move silently out

1

of my room, she hears me each and every morning. So now, at least until my son returns home, I have a companion joining me for my quiet morning hours of precious solitude.

I allowed her in the sitting room under one very strict condition: that she say nothing to me during our time in the room together. She's kept her word, but I may have to be the one to break our agreement. I'm not sure I can stand to sit across from her much longer. Not knowing what she's thinking while she looks at me is driving me mad.

She thinks I'm so enthralled by the snowfall outside that I'm unaware of the look in her eyes. She's wrong. I've lived in Scotland my entire life. More specifically, I've lived in this part of Scotland —this very castle—since I was fourteen. It snows almost every day in this part of the country during winter, so I've seen my fair share of snow. While it is quite stunning with the way it falls around the pond and slowly turns the water to a frozen blanket of ice, beauty isn't the reason I sit in my favorite chair, by my favorite fireplace at the same time every day to look through the frosted window. I sit here because if I situate myself early enough, just as the sun begins to come up, I get to listen to the castle come awake. To hear my many grandchildren begin to stir, to hear their tired mothers and spoiled fathers start their day fills my heart with gratitude.

There was a time—a long time—after Niall died that I wasn't sure I would ever be capable of feeling any positive emotion ever again.

While I was now on the other side of such pain, it had been the battle of my life surviving it. The confusion and guilt I'd felt almost killed me, for how can a mother reconcile knowing that her son is a murderer? But the moment I watched another of my beloved sons leave to fight for his own life centuries ahead of me, I knew that giving in to my grief wasn't an option. There was still purpose to my life, still people that needed me, still love to be found. While Eoghanan was away, I'd barricaded myself away and fought—fought through the emotions, fought through the anger, fought through the soul-crushing grief.

Those closest to me allowed me the space I needed to rant and rage and live like a vagabond near my son's grave. I spent weeks wading through the hurt. There were days I was sure it would never end, that I would drown in a pool of my own tears, that my heart would quite literally break in two. Some days I even begged for it to, for then the pain would truly be over. But it didn't. And with time, I found peace.

There was nothing I could've done in the raising of my son or in my loving of him that could've prevented his actions. While I raised two sons that are better men than I could've ever dreamed they would be, there was never anything to be done for Niall. His actions weren't my fault. I couldn't have saved Baodan's first wife. I couldn't have saved my sister. I bore no responsibility for Niall's acts of murder.

Of course, it took me a long time to see the evil inside him. It took me even longer to acknowledge it. Mothers love their children beyond all reason—we will fight for them, die for them, and we almost always believe the best of them.

It was the darkest time of my life, but now I was truly afraid of nothing. The worst had already happened to me, and I survived. If there was a blessing to be found in anything that happened, that was it.

Mitsy coughed quietly to my left and I turned to see her still staring in my direction. I truly couldn't stand it any longer.

"Mitsy, I said ye couldna speak to me if ye sat in here, but yer eyes have been screaming at me for days. What is it?"

She blinked for what seemed like the first time in hours as her cheeks flushed a red that nearly matched the shade of her hair.

"I don't know what you mean. I wasn't staring at you—just through you. I think I was half-asleep."

Crossing my legs and pulling the blanket that lay across my lap up a little higher, I shook my head in denial.

3

"What is that foul phrase that ye and Jane are so fond of—bullshit? Aye, that is it. Ye are full of it, Mitsy. Ye are wide awake. What is it ye've been wishing to say to me for days?"

"You need more, Kenna."

"More?" While I always found much of what Mitsy said to be perplexing—her twenty-first century phrasing and language often conflicted with my seventeenth century language—I hadn't the slightest idea what she meant this time. "More? Lass, look around. I live in one of the finest castles in Scotland. I've not known a day of poverty in my life. I doona know what it feels like to go hungry. I know few who are as fortunate."

Mitsy said nothing as she stood and lifted her chair. Carrying it until it sat right beside my own, she returned to her seat, faced me, and reached forward to gather my hands in hers.

"You're right. Most people would be perfectly content to have the life that you do, but you're not most people. You know as well as I do that you can both be grateful for what you have and still want more. If you didn't believe that, you wouldn't constantly be encouraging everyone around you to go after the things they want. You're bored here, Kenna. You need some adventure."

"Adventure?" I laughed as imaginings of me crawling aboard a ship and sailing to new land crossed my mind. I'd be so seasick in a day that I'd want to throw myself overboard. I was too old for adventure. "Mitsy, lassies as old as me doona wish for adventure. All we want are quiet mornings, early dinners, and a good night's sleep."

Mitsy withdrew her hands and crossed her arms defiantly.

"Bullshit. Bullshit on all counts."

"There ye go with that language again. Is it truly necessary?"

"Ha. That's rich, Kenna. You've a filthier mouth than the old man who owns the tavern in the village. You just curse in Gaelic rather than English so it sounds more pleasant."

Guiltily, I glanced down. She was right. "Ach, mayhap so. It doesna matter. Get on with it."

Mitsy smiled and held up one finger. "First of all, you aren't old. You're barely past fifty." She lifted one more finger. "Second, I feel quite sure a huge portion of people in their fifties would be quite offended by your little statement of what 'people your age' want. I know you, Kenna. You would love for your days to be a little less predictable, you would love to get to experience firsthand just a little bit of the magic so many of your family members now take for granted."

I'd never said any such thing out loud, but I couldn't deny that she was right. Magic surrounded my family. Magic had been the single force that had helped both of my sons find the women they loved—magic, and the meddling witch, Morna. I was grateful to her for all she'd done for my family but so far I'd experienced little such magic myself. I was more than a little curious to see what it would be like to spend some time in another century.

When I said nothing, Mitsy continued.

"I think you should get out of town for a little bit—go with Cooper when he leaves at the end of the weekend. He'd love to have you along, and I'm sure Morna wouldn't mind the extra house guest."

"No." I dismissed her suggestion immediately. December was the busiest time of year at McMillan Castle. There were celebrations to prepare for, villagers to assist during the cold weather, and grandchildren that expected me to uphold our annual Christmas traditions.

"No?" The enthusiasm waned from Mitsy's voice. She'd not expected such a firm refusal. "You don't want to at least discuss the idea a little bit?"

Smiling, I softened my expression and leaned forward to pat her knee.

"I know ye mean well, Mitsy, but there's no need to discuss this. It wouldna be a good idea."

"And why exactly is that? I guarantee you that for every reason you give me as to why you shouldn't do this, I can give you ten

5

reasons why you should. Come on then, give me your first excuse."

Aggravated, I stood and stepped closer to the fire as I reached up and placed one hand on the mantle.

"I doona need many excuses. My first is good enough. While young Cooper may be able to survive a quick dip in the freezing pond at this time of year, I would surely fall ill and die."

I could never make any sense of Morna's method of time travel here at McMillan Castle. Everyone who traveled forward or backward through time ended up splashing around in the castle pond upon arrival in their new time. It was an unnecessarily rough entry after a very long trip.

Mitsy laughed and moved to stand next to me by the fireplace.

"Nice try. You know as well as I do that she's changed that."

I was entirely unaware of the change. "I can assure ye, I've heard of no such thing."

"What? You experienced it yourself. The way we all went forward for Kamden and Harper's wedding—via the West tower of the castle—it's as simple as that now. No more rock throwing, no more swimming in the lake. Cooper's getting a little older now, and she wanted to make it easier for him to make the trip on his own."

The wedding of my twenty-first century descendent was the only time I'd traveled into the future. I'd seen many wondrous things, but much to my dismay, I'd had no time to explore them— I'd not even had the time to travel beyond the castle grounds.

"Oh. I assumed the witch only made an exception the one time since there were so many of us going forward at once."

Mitsy shook her head and smiled. "Nope. What's your next excuse?"

"I..." I hesitated. I wasn't sure, but I knew there must be some other reason I couldn't go—even as much as I might secretly want to. "I'll not deny that I'm tempted by yer suggestion, Mitsy, but I would make an awful fool of myself in yer time. I've nothing to wear, I doona know how things work, and Cooper shouldna spend his time with Morna explaining every little thing to me."

Little footsteps approached the doorway and Mitsy and I both turned to see early-riser Cooper burst through the door.

"Did you ask her yet? What'd she say?"

Winking at me, Mitsy faced Cooper.

"She's undecided. I think she needs you to convince her."

He ran toward me as quickly as his little feet would carry him, and I opened my arms to catch him as he jumped up and into my arms. He was growing quickly. I wouldn't be able to pick him up much longer. Until that sad day came, I would hold him anytime he wished me too.

"Come on, Nana. Anything that you're worried about, we've got a plan for. I promise. I know you're nervous, but it would be so much fun. I'd love for you to come with me."

Excitement like I'd not felt in years blossomed within me as I gave myself permission to do something unexpected.

"Are ye sure, Cooper? I know ye enjoy yer time with Morna. I wouldna wish to intrude."

"Are you kidding? Morna would love it. And so would I. Please, Nana. Come with me."

Mitsy reached her hand up to tussle the top of Cooper's wavy curls. She'd known all along that the moment Cooper was in on the plan, I wouldn't be able to say no.

"Kenna, if I can promise you that we'll get you everything you need, that we will prepare you in every way, will you do it?"

"If ye will make certain I willna make a fool of myself, then aye, I'll go."

Cooper squirmed out of my arms and grabbed onto Mitsy's hand to pull her out of the room. Turning to look back at me over his shoulder, he smiled at me as they left.

"Don't you worry, Nana. We've got everything under control."

That was exactly what I was worried about.

CHAPTER 2

*C*hicago – *Present Day*

*M*alcolm Warren looked forward to the last day of
school before Christmas break every year. It
meant two full weeks with his daughter and granddaughter as they
enjoyed their annual trip to Scotland to visit his brother and
sister-in-law. This year would be especially festive, for at fifty-
eight years young, he was an uncle for the very first time.

Rosalind was excited, too. With his window rolled down so he
could wave to her from in front of the school, she started talking
to him before she even got in the car.

"Will the baby be walking yet? Do you think Emilia will let me
hold him?"

"Hello to you too, kiddo. Get in the car before you freeze to
death. I think it's colder here in Chicago than it will be in
Scotland."

Once Rosalind was safely inside the car with her seatbelt

fastened, Malcolm answered his granddaughter's insistent questions.

"The baby won't be walking, though I expect he will be crawling all over the place. And of course Emilia will let you hold him. You'll be a big help to her. How was the last day of school?"

Rolling her eyes, the young girl huffed and shook her head.

"It was a total waste of time. This whole week was. It was all parties and Christmas crafts. What am I doing in school if not to do some real learning? I would've been better off just leaving for Scotland a week early."

Malcolm smiled to himself as he drove the short distance to the home they all shared.

"You know, most kids like the days when there's less school work."

She glanced over at him, giving him a smile identical to her mother's, and Malcolm's heart squeezed. His girls were his world. They would never know how much either of them meant to him.

"Pops, have I ever been like most kids?"

"No, and that's one of your best qualities. Most kids drive me crazy."

Rosalind laughed as he pulled into the driveway.

"I know you try to seem grumpier than you are, but nobody buys it. You like everybody."

It was true. While his stature might be intimidating, Malcolm knew his heart was softer than most men he knew. He was an incurable sap.

"Some people buy it. I can be grumpy when I need to be."

Rosalind ignored him as she opened the car door and stepped outside. He knew immediately from the way her eyes darted over to the tightly shut garage door she'd just noticed what he'd already seen—her mother still wasn't home.

"She's not here, Pops. I knew this was going to happen. I just knew it."

Malcolm hurried to place a reassuring hand on his

granddaughter's shoulder as he guided her up the front steps to their home.

"Don't worry yet, Rosie. She could just be stuck in traffic. We don't know that she had to work late."

Shoulders slumped, head down, the young girl leaned into him as he worked to open the front door.

"She always has to work late. We're going to miss our flight."

"Don't you worry about that—we still have an hour or so before we have to be at the airport. We are not going to miss our flight. I'll call the hospital right now. Why don't you go and pack the last of your things and bring your bag downstairs? We can get the car loaded while we wait on her."

Waiting until Rosalind disappeared at the top of the stairs, Malcolm closed the door and made his way into the kitchen. Pulling out his phone, he saw the notification he dreaded might be there—a voicemail from his daughter.

Turning the volume down low so Rosie wouldn't hear it—he could hear her lingering on the stairs—he pressed play and held the phone up to his ear.

"Hey Dad. Look, I know you guys aren't going to be happy with me, and I really hate to do this, but I simply can't leave the hospital right now. Half the nursing staff is trying to take off, and I have too many patients who need me. You guys go ahead and leave for Scotland. I'll catch a flight out sometime next week. I'll definitely be there by Christmas. Tell Rosie that I love her. I love you too, Dad. Oh, and Dad. Don't call the hospital. I don't have time to discuss this with either of you. Just leave and have a great first day in Edinburgh. I'll meet you guys there soon. Bye."

Rosalind entered the kitchen before he had time to call for her.

"I guess I shouldn't bring Mom's bags down? I can tell by your face that she isn't coming."

"I'm so sorry, sweetheart. She's just too swamped..."

"No!" Rosalind's angry voice interrupted him as tears began to swell in her eyes. Her knees wobbled as she gripped the doorway.

"Don't make excuses for her. Not anymore. She always acts like she has a good reason, but there's no good reason for this."

Malcolm couldn't argue with her. He knew the pain his daughter was in all too well, but it didn't give her permission to abandon her daughter. For the better part of two years, she'd closed herself off from all life outside the hospital, and it was Rosalind who suffered for it.

Moving across the room, Malcolm dropped to his knees and reached to wrap his arms around Rosie. She buried her head in his neck and cried.

"You're right. I won't. I know there have been lots of times that she hasn't been there for you since your father passed away, but this time she's gone too far. This isn't right or fair. I'm as angry with her as I've ever been. But this is Christmas, and I refuse to let her ruin it for you."

Ripping herself away from him, Rosalind picked up her bag and stormed through the front door of the house.

"She already has. Now, let's get this stupid show on the road."

Anger always caused Rosie to lash out at those around her. Only in the car for a few seconds, she began to honk the horn at him, fire in her eyes as he dragged his own bag outside and locked the front door.

The young girl was heartbroken and angry, and he would pay the price for it.

Malcolm could sense with every fiber of his being that his beloved granddaughter would give him hell during every second of their trip to Scotland.

CHAPTER 3

*M*cMillan Castle – 1651

"Y ou've no reason to be nervous, Kenna. From the first moment I met you, I knew you were a woman far ahead of your time. Much like Mitsy and Grace were born in another time but belong in this one, I've always wondered if perhaps you belonged in theirs."

I turned toward Bebop in surprise as we continued our morning walk. It was a ritual we started almost immediately after his arrival in the seventeenth century. Each morning, shortly after breakfast, we would meet in the castle's garden where, no matter the weather, we would walk for over an hour. It was good exercise for us both, and over the years we'd become the best of friends.

"Why would ye say that? I've never felt that way myself."

"Well, for starters, you don't think like most people born and raised in this time. Kenna, you are as open-minded as they come. And perhaps you've never felt that way yourself because you've never spent time in another century. I won't be surprised if you have no desire to come back after a few weeks away."

"I'll want to come back. There are far too many people here who I love to stay away."

Bebop reached over to squeeze my shoulder. "And that, my dear, is the only reason I believe you will come back"

"Do ye truly believe I'll love it so much?"

"I do. This isn't exactly related to the subject at hand, but would you like a good laugh?"

I would never say no to that.

"O'course, I do."

"We both know Cooper regularly asks interesting questions. There is nothing the young boy won't say or ask, but this question surprised even me, and I'm rarely surprised by anything."

My curiosity piqued, I took one step closer to him as we walked.

"What did he ask ye?"

"He asked when the two of us were going to get married."

"Wha...what...whatever gave him that idea?" I felt like the air had suddenly been kicked from my chest. It was the most ridiculous suggestion I'd ever heard.

Bebop shook his head as he chuckled softly.

"I haven't the slightest idea. I guess he just assumed that since we are both his grandparents now and both of our spouses are gone that we should naturally be together."

"Oh. Well, I suppose if I were seven years old, I might think as he does. What did ye say to him?"

"Firstly, I explained to him that despite my youthful appearance." He paused to chuckle at himself. "I was significantly older than you. Then, I went on to tell him that anyone who knows my real name and still calls me 'Bebop,' probably doesn't have any romantic inclinations for me."

"And do ye have them for me? I know that ye doona."

"I would be lucky to have you, Kenna, but no, you are the

dearest friend I have here, and I wouldn't want to do anything to ruin that."

"Good." I pointed up ahead where our anticipated guests were approaching the castle. "They're here."

Mitsy's closest friend, Bri, her husband, and their children, along with Bri's mother, Adelle and her husband, Hew, were coming to stay with us for Christmas. Adelle, as I'd learned shortly after Cooper's warning that they had a plan for everything, had already been assigned to help me prepare for my time in the future.

Bebop picked up his pace and reached his hand behind to wave me forward.

"We best hurry then. I've not been around Adelle too much, but I know she has a penchant for talking. You and Cooper leave this evening and I expect she will have a week's worth of information to tell you. Best you get started soon."

Nerves and excitement gathered in equal measure in my chest as I marched toward my first lesson on how to survive in the twenty-first century.

I had just fastened myself into my first-ever bra when both my daughters-in-law, Grace and Mitsy, burst into the room where Adelle and I were picking modern outfits for me to pack from her wide selection.

Mitsy gazed unabashedly at my chest for a matter of seconds and then turned to address Adelle.

"Nice. You're a little bit taller, Adelle, but other than that, you two are just about the same size."

"We are. Lucky thing too since much to my dismay the rest of you girls have let your collection of modern clothes dwindle over the years."

Grace laughed and passed a white button-down blouse in my direction.

"We don't really need them anymore. Why go to the hassle of keeping things that we don't wear handy?"

"You girls must be more evolved than I am. Don't get me wrong. I love my life here, but the fashion of this time doesn't suit my tastes at all. I don't really wear them anymore, but sometimes just looking at my old clothes makes me happy. I'm thrilled they will finally be getting some use."

The buttons on the blouse felt strange beneath my fingers. While the clothes were undoubtedly more comfortable, I felt uncomfortable in them—exposed and wholly unlike myself.

Grace came to stand behind me in the mirror and leaned in close while Adelle and Mitsy began discussing what they missed most about life in the twenty-first century. They were split between hot baths and microwavable popcorn.

"It will take some getting used to, but once you do, you'll love this way of dressing. And if it makes you feel any better now, you look absolutely gorgeous. How does the makeup feel? Do you think you can manage it yourself?"

"Thank ye, Grace." I reached up to gently brush at my newly blackened lashes. "It feels less odd than I expected. Aye, I think I can manage. Adelle took her time showing me how to apply it, though I refused much of what she offered me." Adelle had shoved an entire satchel full of makeup toward me but I only ended up setting aside four items to pack—all of which were entirely new to me: a light powder, eyeliner, mascara, and a burgundy-colored lipstick.

"What you have on is perfect. You don't need much. You're stunning without anything on. I can hear my youngest screaming in the other room so I can't stay away long, but I wanted to come in here and tell you something while it was on my mind. I know that you're going *with* Cooper but I don't want you to feel like you are going to *care for* Cooper. He's stayed alone with Morna and Jerry many times. I trust them with my son completely. What I'm saying is, don't use Cooper as an excuse not to get out and explore while you're there. I want you to soak up everything there is to see, to seize every opportunity that comes your way. You deserve this. You deserve some time away. You deserve some fun. Okay? Promise me you won't feel the need to stay with Cooper every second."

Turning away from the mirror to face her, I reached my arms around Grace to hug her close.

"Thank ye. Having ye tell me that yerself will certainly make me more likely to do so. Are ye coming to see the two of us off?"

McMillan Castle's youngest babe let out an ear-piercing scream and Grace stiffened in my arms.

"Yes, of course. I want to squeeze both of you before you go. Now, however, I must go see to that. Eoghanan is good for many, many things but comforting crying babies isn't one of them."

Grace left, followed shortly by Mitsy, leaving Adelle and me to pack up the rest of my borrowed belongings alone.

"Grace is right, you know. You need to take full advantage of your time there. With Morna involved, it's bound to be a wonderful time for you. Do you mind if I give you my own piece of advice—one grandmother to another?"

Cooper and I would leave within the hour. Everything was real now, and I could no longer hide my apprehension.

"I consider myself to be a rather strong woman, but the closer I get to leaving, the more nauseous I feel. I'll take any advice ye can give me, Adelle."

"Great. And just so you know, I'm only saying something because Grace told me how you sent her to Eoghanan's room before they were married, so I know you're secretly a modern-minded lady like myself. Otherwise, I wouldn't risk offending you."

I laughed and reached to squeeze Adelle's hand. "I canna remember the last time I was offended by anything."

"That's really good. Okay, I can tell by your complexion that it's been a really long time since you've had a good lay. If I know Morna at all, she will see to it that the opportunity arises while you are with her to fix that. Do it. Forget about all of the rules of propriety that apply to things here. Things are very different in the twenty-first century. Have the sex. Eat the cake. Drink the extra glass of wine. Let your hair down a bit."

Whatever I'd expected her to say, it hadn't been that.

"Ye can tell by my complexion?" The thought horrified me.

She shrugged. "What can I say? It's always been my superpower. Now, let's get you to Cooper so the two of you can head out."

Laughing, I lifted the handle of my modern roller bag and then leaned playfully into Adelle.

"Do ye know what, Adelle? I know that I doona know ye verra well, but I already know that I like ye verra much."

Smiling, she wrapped her arm around my shoulder as we left the room.

"I like you too, Kenna. I'm totally serious, though. When you guys return in two weeks, I expect your face to be glowing. Glowing from all the sex."

"Aye, I understood what ye meant by glowing from yer first reference to my ruddy complexion."

She nodded. "Just driving the point home."

"I believe ye did. I shall endeavor to return home all aglow."

Laughing like lassies half our age, we made our way to the castle's west tower together.

CHAPTER 4

O n The Road to Conall Castle, Scotland – Present Day

I f Rosalind sighed any louder, the tourists in the very back of the bus would be able to hear her. It was now three days into their trip and with no word from Rosie's mother, the young girl's mood continued to decline.

Listening to the young girl cry herself to sleep had been the deciding factor for Malcolm. Staying in his brother's home where they all had so many shared memories of Christmases together only seemed to make matters worse for his granddaughter. It only reminded her that during a time of year when both of her parents should be there, neither of them were.

There was no need for them to stay in Edinburgh for the entire trip. Perhaps it would do Rosalind some good to get out of the house and explore the country a bit. They could travel for a few days and then return to Edinburgh for the real Christmas celebrations.

Unable to sleep from the soft sounds of Rosie crying inside

her room, Malcolm had arranged a weekend getaway in which they would explore a bit of the Highlands. And now, only twelve hours after the decision was made, they were aboard a bus, enjoying the three-hour scenic drive from Edinburgh to the first stop on their trip—Conall Castle.

At least he was enjoying the drive. So far, the diversion wasn't working for Rosie.

"This is the castle you wanted to see, isn't it? I was almost certain this was the one you mentioned to me before."

Rosalind didn't face him as she answered. Instead, she kept her gaze focused out the bus window to her left.

"Mom and I planned to see it together. We can just add this to the long list of things she's missed."

"We can always come and visit it again when she gets here."

Rosalind turned slowly toward him, her eyes red and teary. Her eyes and nose were beginning to look raw from all the crying. Malcolm needed to find some way to make the child smile.

"Don't you know it by now, Pops? She isn't coming. Last Christmas was just too hard on her. I know she hasn't said it yet, but I know her. She won't be here for Christmas."

Malcolm worried that his granddaughter was right. Tim had loved Christmas so much. His daughter seemed incapable of celebrating the holiday now that he was gone.

"It won't always be this way, Rosie. Sometimes, grief takes a very long time to work through. She will find her way back to you."

Taking a deep breath in through her nose, Rosalind turned away from him and stared out the window once more. He could see Conall Castle in the distance through the front window of the bus. They were almost there.

"Let's not talk about your mother anymore today. Let's just try and enjoy this time together."

As the bus pulled to a stop and the castle's guide stepped aboard the bus to welcome them, Malcolm turned his attention to the tour. One by one they got off the bus and followed the perky and knowledgeable guide along the short trail leading up to the castle's main doors.

While he was certain Rosalind had followed him off the bus, he turned to whisper to her halfway through the tour and found her no longer behind him. Frantically, his gaze tore through their group. She was gone. Rosalind was nowhere to be found.

M cMillan Castle – Present Day

"*A* ch, Cooper, does it always hurt so much?" I gripped my head painfully as we slowly moved down the tower stairwell into the twenty-first century version of my home.

The method of travel was simple enough. All we needed was for Cooper to open his magical pocket watch, ask Morna to bring us forward, and in a flash we disappeared, only to reappear in the exact same location seconds later, centuries ahead of the time we left. As simple as it was, the magic's effects on my body could be felt all over. I was disoriented, and while my body ached everywhere, nothing hurt as badly as my head.

"Don't worry, Nana. Harper keeps some ibuprofen handy. She'll have it waiting for you."

I was mildly aware of modern medicines. My daughters-in-law kept several pills and tinctures hidden away for times when illness befell anyone in the castle that a simple herbal mixture wouldn't cure.

"Only for me? Does yer head not hurt?"

The young boy shrugged and bounded down the stairs ahead of me.

"Nope. The more you do it, the easier it gets. Plus, you're old so that probably has something to do with why you feel so bad."

Shaking my head, I met up with him as he waited at the bottom of the stairs for me.

"I believe we need to have a discussion about my actual age. Several instances as of late have given me reason to believe ye think me far more ancient than I am."

Cooper smiled and let out a quick giggle.

"I'm only teasing you, Nana. You're not old. You don't look it anyway."

"Thank ye. Now, where is this ibuprofen?"

"It's right here."

I looked up to see Harper, the wife of my descendent and the true leader of McMillan Castle in the twenty-first century. She was energetic, organized, and without her my home would've fallen into disrepair long ago. I gratefully accepted the pills and glass of water she extended in my direction.

"Neither of you look too worse for wear. You'll be pleased to know that Jerry is already here. He's got the car all warmed up for you."

"He's here already?" Cooper's voice couldn't have sounded any more excited. "We left our bags in the tower. Let me go and get them so we can get to Morna's."

Harper reached out a hand to stop him.

"Don't worry about that. Kamden will gather up your bags. I told Sileas you were coming this morning, and he's been wagging his tail all morning with excitement. Why don't you go and say hello to him and leave your things to my husband?"

The castle dog, Sileas, was almost taller than Cooper when standing on all fours, but the sweet beast collapsed on the ground and rolled over onto his back like a small puppy the moment Cooper neared him.

With Cooper occupied, Harper hooked her arm with my own and walked with me outside to the car.

"I'm glad you decided to come, Kenna. It will be good for you."

Still nervous, my voice was much more shaky than I wished it to be as I answered her. "That's what everyone keeps saying. I hope all of ye are right."

"We are." She leaned in to hug me and kiss my cheek as Jerry stepped out of the car to greet me. "Christmas is the most magical time of year. I can't wait to see what happens to you over the next few weeks."

---

*M*y first car ride was thrilling. While Cooper slept restfully in the back seat of Jerry's very tiny car, I happily sat next to Jerry in the front as I delighted in the swirl of scenery that changed every second.

"Ye are going to be fun for all of us, lass. I can tell."

I knew smiling for hours was a bit much, but I truly couldn't stop. Everything outside the car window was amazing. With all of the means of travel I was accustomed to, it would've taken days to see what we'd seen in three hours of driving.

"What do ye mean?"

"Yer excitement is contagious. 'Tis always a joy to watch another experience something for the first time. It has been far too long since we've enjoyed the company of a newbie to this time."

While I could discern the meaning of the word *newbie* by its context well enough, it was a word I'd never heard before in my life.

"How far away are we?"

Cooper's sleepy voice spoke to us from behind and I twisted to look at him.

"I doona care if it takes us all night to get there. I never expected a ride in a car to be so pleasurable."

Out of the corner of my eye, I could see Jerry lift one hand from the wheel and point ahead of him.

"We are nearly there now. I'm turning onto the dirt road which leads to Conall Castle and our inn as we speak."

I faced the front to see the faint outline of the castle in the distance, but there was something else along the road ahead, a faint outline of a creature or a person walking along the road's outer edge.

"Look, guys—it's a girl!"

I leaned forward and strained to make out the form Cooper pointed at. Sure enough, a girl who couldn't be more than a few years older than Cooper, walked all alone ahead of us.

CHAPTER 5

I liked the strange girl instantly, despite her rather unfriendly demeanor. I recognized the look in her eyes —the grief and the anger that was so potently felt, she no longer tried to hide it at all. Not so long ago, I'd been there myself. She also had a defiantly independent nature that I appreciated in any woman, but most especially in someone so young. Despite having so much growth ahead of her, she already knew herself more than many women ever do.

"Look, sir, I appreciate you offering me a ride, but I don't know you. There's no way I'm getting into that car with you."

Jerry, accustomed to willful women, was unbothered by the young girl's refusal. He remained patient, calm, and insistent as he tried to reason with her. Cooper and I watched on in silence, enjoying the exchange.

"Lassie, 'twould be improper for me to leave a child stranded along a dirt road. 'Tis at least a mile back to the castle. I'll not do it. If ye willna get in this car, I shall follow along beside ye until either whoever ye are with finds ye or yer legs give out from exhaustion. 'Tis snowing and ye are near soaked through. Ye've no hat on yer head, no muffs on yer ears, and no gloves that I can see. When we do find whoever ye are with, I shall scold them for allowing ye out of doors without anything to keep ye warm."

"Watch it, old man." There was fire in the girl's tone. Something that Jerry had said made her immediately defensive. "You'll say nothing to my grandfather. It's not his fault that I ignored him."

Jerry smiled and cast me a quick glance.

"Ah. Thank ye, lass. We are finally making some progress. At least I now know who ye are with. Is yer grandfather back at the castle? If so, why doona ye get in the back with Cooper and we will drive ye to him?"

The young girl pointed to Cooper in the back seat who responded by waving at her. She rolled her eyes in response.

"How do I know that you didn't kidnap that little boy in the back and now you want to kidnap me, too?"

Cooper quickly protested by rolling down his window and sticking his head outside to speak to the girl directly.

"I am *not* that little. And Jerry hasn't kidnapped me. I'd like to see someone try to take me if I didn't want to go."

Quietly, so the girl outside couldn't hear him, Jerry leaned back and whispered over his shoulder to Cooper.

"I'm not sure if I'd be so confident about that, lad. It did already happen once before if ye doona remember?"

On impulse, I reached out and hit Jerry softly on the arm. The very memory of the old witch who'd taken Cooper from us once before made my blood boil. I tried my best to block it from my memory. I was certain Cooper tried to do the same.

The girl laughed and crossed her arms, leaning back onto her heels.

"Only someone really little would feel the need to tell me how 'not little' they are."

Cooper's face flushed red as he sank back inside the car.

Jerry laughed and attempted to divert the conversation back toward him.

"There. Cooper has told ye himself that he is not kidnapped. If ye truly doona wish to get in this car, then fine, turn yerself around and walk back toward the castle. I'll follow behind ye to make certain ye get there safely."

I could see by the flash in the young girl's eyes that she saw this as a victory. Without a word she turned and marched off in front of the car.

I leaned over and spoke softly to Jerry—not that she could hear me from outside the car anyway.

"Ye really are going to have to follow her all the way. She's strong-willed. She doesna wish to give in to ye."

Jerry nodded and pressed on the brake as he turned to address Cooper.

"Aye, I know. Cooper, what should we do? Ye know women well."

I wasn't all together sure how true that was, but I could see by the way Cooper lifted in his seat that Jerry's confidence in him was just what he needed after the girl's insult. It wouldn't hurt to let Cooper think of an idea to try.

Cooper smiled and unbuckled his seatbelt. "I know just the thing, guys. Just give me some space, okay?"

We both nodded and allowed Cooper to get out of the car. Rolling down my own window, I urged Jerry to do the same.

"Open all the windows and pull up beside them rather than behind. I wish to hear what they are saying to one another."

Jerry obeyed without question.

"What are you doing? I don't know you either, little boy. You need to get back in your car and leave me alone."

Cooper carried himself tall and didn't shrink at the girl's cold welcome. Instead, he moved to block her path and extended his hand.

"You could at least say hello to me. My name's Cooper, what's your name?"

Forced to stop, the young girl eyed him suspiciously. Cautiously, she extended her hand.

"Rosalind." She hesitated and then added, "but most people call me Rosie."

I smiled as Cooper shook her hand and moved out of her way, falling in step beside her as she continued her march back toward the castle. The name suited her. Significantly taller than Cooper, the girl was slender and pale with very short strawberry-blonde hair that fell much more in the realm of strawberry than blonde. Her eyes were jade green, and the smattering of freckles across her face would, one day when she was older, be stunning.

It was unusual in my time to see a female with such short hair, but I quite liked it. It fit the young girl's personality perfectly. Eager to see what Cooper would do next, I watched on.

"It's really cold out here, ya know?"

Rosie nodded but didn't look over at Cooper as she walked.

"Yes, I do know. Maybe you should get back in the car with the old man and the woman who keeps staring at me."

I shrunk slightly back in my seat but didn't look away at her words.

Cooper shook his head.

"Nope. As long as you're walking, I'm going to walk next to you. And, as you said, I'm little and it's very, very cold out here. I might get sick."

To emphasize this, Cooper coughed rather dramatically into his arm.

Rosalind stopped cold, crossed her arms as she'd done before and looked at him.

"You people are crazy. I don't like any of you one bit."

Cooper grinned. He could see that he was succeeding.

"We're just trying to help you."

Turning, she stomped away from him and opened the car door before crawling inside.

"I don't need anybody's help. The second we get back to the castle and I find my grandfather, I don't want to see any of you guys ever again."

Jerry laughed and sped up as we barreled toward the castle.

"Verra well, lass, but see ye to yer grandfather, we shall."

CHAPTER 6

*W*hen Malcolm saw the old, rickety car pull up to the front of Conall Castle, the terror that had gripped him for the better part of an hour melted away in a rush. He could see Rosalind's red hair through the window, and his knees nearly gave way as relief washed over him. While he'd known she couldn't have gone far—there was only one road leading to the castle—he'd been terrified.

Running outside to meet her, he gathered her up in his arms and dropped to his knees.

"Where on earth did you go?"

Rosalind was stiff in his grip. With a muffled voice, she spoke into the front of his shirt.

"You've got to let go of me, Pops. I can't breathe. I didn't go anywhere. I was just bored to death on the tour and thought I'd walk around a little while. I was just walking down the road."

It was only when he released her and stood that he took notice of the old man standing on the other side of the car. While it took him a moment to recognize him—it had been at least five years since he'd seen him—he knew as soon as he heard the man's voice that it was Jerry.

"Malcolm! Why, I dinna know Rosie was yer granddaughter. Had I known, I wouldna have been so patient with her. How are ye, man? 'Tis been far too long since ye visited these parts."

The snow now fell in a heavy blanket over them. As he leaned forward to hug Jerry, he could see Rosie trembling beside them from the cold. She was wet all the way through.

"I'm much better now. Thank you for picking her up."

"O'course. I was on my way back home when we spotted her. I dinna know who she belonged to, but I couldna verra well leave her out in the snow."

Noticing the castle's tour guide a few yards away, Malcolm reached for Rosie's hand.

"Jerry, it's good to see you, but I'm afraid we must both get back to the group. Rosie delayed everyone long enough by wandering off and the entire group has been searching for her. I need to let them know she's back."

Just as he began to step away, Jerry reached and grabbed his arm.

"By all means, let them know the lass is safe but then why doona the two of ye gather yer bags from the bus and come with me back to the inn for the night? Morna would never forgive me if she found out that I bumped into ye and then dinna bring ye back to the house so she could see ye."

Malcolm couldn't deny the appeal of Jerry's suggestion. Rosalind needed to get dry, and Morna and Jerry's inn was undoubtedly closer than the tour group's next stop.

"We wouldn't be intruding?"

Jerry waved a dismissive hand.

"Not at all. I promise ye, my wife would insist on it if she were here so I must do so on her behalf. Rosie can wait in the car for ye while ye gather yer things."

Seeing his granddaughter inside the car, he leaned in close to whisper in her ear before leaving to retrieve their things.

"When we get to the inn, we will discuss this further."

*W*hile she said nothing, it was evident that Rosalind was near tears as she waited for her grandfather. Her breathing was tight, and I could see her reddened cheeks from the mirror outside my window.

Jerry and Cooper could sense the tension in the young girl, as well, and we remained quiet as we waited for the man I now knew was named Malcolm to return with their belongings.

When he began his walk back toward the car, I was able to get a clear view of him for the first time.

He was one of the most handsome men I'd ever seen. As tall as both of my sons, I would be dwarfed in size if I stood next to him. His hair was very dark and thick, slightly unruly, and much like my own, it had begun to gray in mixed places throughout. His blue eyes stood out from amongst his mass of black hair, and he had the sort of scruffy facial hair that made it look as if he were in the beginning stages of trying to grow it out. Although, I expected that with all of the fascinating tools I knew existed in the twenty-first century, that he kept it trimmed that way all the time.

I didn't realize he'd stopped walking and that we were both staring at one another until his knuckles lightly rapped on my closed window. Startled, I jerked back as my cheeks warmed in embarrassment. I was certain they were now as red as Rosie's.

"I'm so sorry to ask you this," Malcolm straightened and swept his hand downward in a motion meant to emphasize the length of his legs. "I don't think I'll fit in the back seat. Would you mind switching with me?"

There was no question that if he attempted to sit in the back, he would be forced to sit in a terribly uncomfortable position, if he could manage to fit in the back at all.

"Oh. Aye, o'course." Fumbling with the door handle, I

eventually managed to clumsily step outside. When I righted myself, Malcolm extended me his hand.

"I hate to have you move. I'm Malcolm, but you can call me Mac, most people do."

He had quite possibly the largest hands I'd ever seen. I found them to be wildly attractive.

Strong yet gentle, his fingers were long and masculine. The touch of them against my own as he slid his hand around mine made my knees wobbly in a way that both shocked and horrified me.

"'Tis no trouble at all, I assure ye. I...I'm Kenna. Ye may call me Kenna." It was a ridiculous thing to say, and the smile that spread across his face at my words made me want to disappear into the snow.

"Very well. It's a pleasure to meet you, Kenna. Here, let me open the door for you."

As he ushered me into the back seat of the car next to a wet and freezing Rosie who was forced to slide over into the middle, his hand touched my back and I gasped. Thankfully, Cooper was the only one who noticed my quick intake of breath, but the oddly perceptive child immediately turned his head away from me to giggle.

The drive back to Morna and Jerry's was short, and as expected, Morna stood outside her home awaiting our arrival.

I was the first one to climb out of the car, and before I managed to say one word of greeting to her, Morna pulled me to her in a tight embrace.

"Ach, lassie. I'm so pleased ye decided to join Cooper." And then, lowering her voice so that no one save me could hear her, she pressed her lips against my ear and whispered. "Our other guests doona know about any of the magic. Best we not tell them."

Raising her voice once more, she pushed me away and moved to gather up Cooper, most assuredly to give him the same warning. Not that it was needed. Everyone who'd ever fallen prey to Morna's meddling magic quickly became accustomed to keeping secrets. Cooper would know not to say anything.

"Cooper, lad. I've missed ye more than ye know. Get yerself over here and give me a hug."

I gathered our belongings as Morna and Cooper hugged. Then I walked over to Jerry so he could direct me.

He attempted to reach for the bags, but I quickly spun them away from him.

"No, thank ye. I can manage both bags just fine, Jerry. Where would ye like me to place them?"

Smiling, Jerry pointed to the top of the stairs.

"Straight up and to yer right there are three rooms. Cooper prefers the room nearest the staircase. Why doona ye take the middle room? Rosie can have the room at the far end."

Nodding, I stepped away. "I'll just place these in our rooms then I'll come downstairs to visit. Thank ye both for letting me stay."

"We are so happy to have ye here, Kenna. We will have plenty of time for conversation. Ye must be exhausted from the journey. If ye get to yer room and feel like resting for a bit, please do so."

By the time I reached my room, my arms ached from fingertip to shoulder from the weight of Cooper's book bag.

The bed looked so inviting.

Surely, a short rest would do no harm.

CHAPTER 7

$\mathcal{I}$ woke to the familiar sound of knuckles lightly rapping. For a few moments upon opening my eyes, I forgot where I was. It was only when I noticed the glow of electric lighting from the side table to my right and the strong smell of food from the kitchen below that everything came flooding back. I was at Morna's—some three hundred plus years ahead of the time I'd been born in.

Pulling myself from the bed, I stood and stretched then nearly fell backwards on the bed once again when I cast a glance out the window to see that the sky was now pitch black. I'd slept for the rest of the day.

The light knock returned. I ran a quick hand through my undoubtedly messy hair and moved to answer it. Expecting Cooper—although, if I were honest with myself, it would've surprised me if he'd actually knocked—I jumped back at the sight of Malcolm standing tall in the doorway.

"Did I wake you? I just saw that the light was on so I thought maybe you weren't sleeping. Forgive me, Kenna. It can wait until morning."

Still drowsy and confused at his presence, I yawned and held up a hand to keep him from leaving.

"No, no. 'Tis fine. I shouldna have slept so long. How far into evening is it?"

He pulled his lips to one side as if he were reluctant to tell me.

"It's close to midnight now. I'm the only one up. I should've assumed that you'd just fallen asleep with the light on, but I saw it and thought perhaps you'd awakened. Now that you're up, are you hungry?"

I found myself unable to remember the last time I'd eaten. The day leading up to my departure had been so filled with preparation and activity, I didn't think I'd stopped once to eat and with all of the traveling today, I knew I'd eaten nothing.

"I'm famished."

"Good. I know I saw Morna stash some leftovers in the fridge. I'll go and warm it up."

Smiling, I nodded and reached for the door.

"Thank ye. Just give me a few moments to fully wake myself and I'll join ye downstairs."

I waited until he disappeared from view before I tip-toed from my room over to the bathroom at the end of the hall. I'd used only one modern toilet in all of my life and to my everlasting embarrassment had been forced to call Mitsy into the room to help me figure out how to work it. To avoid such mortification this time—I'd sooner die than have to call my grandson into the bathroom to educate me on twenty-first century waste removal— I had Adelle give me a thorough lesson on all the new objects I would find in Morna's home.

A mirror hung on the back of the bathroom door, and as I sat down to relieve myself, I caught a glimpse of my reflection. I'd never looked so frightening in all my life. Dark smeared circles surrounded my eyes from smeared mascara. My hair was ratted and smashed drastically to one side. And—worst of all—the top four buttons on the white blouse I was wearing had opened while

I slept. If not for the bra underneath, my breasts would have been totally exposed.

Still, even with the bra, Malcolm had just seen more of my bare chest than any man in the last fifteen years.

---

*E*ven unkempt from sleep, with eyes as dark as raccoons from her makeup, Kenna was stunning. And by God her breasts were perfect. Not that he intentionally looked at her breasts. They'd just been so there, so evident with the way her blouse lay open. He was certain she'd not known. She would be embarrassed when she noticed. Of course, he would say nothing of it. It was best to let her believe that he'd seen nothing below her chin.

The food was already warm and laid out by the time she entered the kitchen. As he expected, her face was now bare, her hair pulled back, and her blouse firmly closed.

"I haven't the slightest idea what this is, but it is delicious. Morna asked me before she went to bed to direct you to the food if you were to wake up hungry during the night."

Kenna's brows pulled together as she sat down in the chair opposite him.

"Why would she tell ye to do that? Does she not expect ye to sleep, as well?"

Malcolm realized that she must've not seen his pallet in the middle of the living room floor on her way to the kitchen.

"She only asked because I'm sleeping in the living room. I suppose she suspected I would wake if anyone came downstairs. Though, she's wrong about that. It always takes me awhile to go to sleep, but once I do, I'm out like a light."

Kenna lifted the fork he'd laid out for her, smiling as she took her first bite of food.

"'Tis shepherd's pie. Quite a delicious one." Speaking between

39

bites of food, she continued. "Malcolm, ye needn't sleep on the floor. I can move my belongings over to Cooper's room and sleep with him."

Malcolm had seen clearly enough the young boy's desire to appear older than he was to his granddaughter. It wouldn't do to have the boy's grandmother sleep with him.

"I wouldn't dream of it. I believe Cooper has taken a bit of a fancy to Rosie. And she already wounded his confidence enough tonight. If she saw that you were sleeping in his room..." he paused and shook his head, "well, I'm not quite sure what this new version of my granddaughter would say to him, but she'd ridicule him for it. The floor suits me just fine. The mattress Morna placed there is honestly quite comfortable."

Malcolm watched as concern crossed Kenna's face. She loved the young boy dearly, and he could see why. Despite Rosie's harsh words, Cooper had been nothing but a delight during their meal. And while he knew Rosie's words must have hurt him, the child had hidden it well.

"What do ye mean? What happened?"

Standing, he went to retrieve a fork for himself before joining in on the other side of the pie.

"That's actually why I came to your room. I just wanted to apologize on behalf of Rosie. She'll be apologizing to Cooper in the morning, I've made sure of that, but I just wanted you to know that how she's behaved since you all met her...well, it's not typical."

Kenna's face softened somewhat and she surprised him by reaching forward to gently lay her hand on top of his. He stilled underneath her touch.

"'Twas Mac ye said I should call ye, aye?"

He nodded.

"Mac, I raised three children and am surrounded by grandchildren almost every day. I know all too well that to judge any child by one day's ill-tempered mood is folly. 'Twas clear to me the moment I saw Rosalind that something had upset her greatly. We all lash out when we are angry. What did she say to him?"

"She asked him if he wanted her to cut up his food since you were sleeping. That surely someone so young couldn't manage by himself."

Kenna's eyes grew wide and Malcolm noticed that he immediately missed her touch as she pulled her hand away and crossed her arms. She didn't look angry at all. If anything, she appeared amused.

"And how did he answer her?"

Malcolm smiled thinking back on the youngster's words.

"He carefully lifted his knife and cut the perfect bite of pie before placing it in his mouth like a gentleman three times his age. Then he looked directly at her and said, 'I think I can manage, but if you have any trouble with your piece, I'll be happy to help you, Rosie. And just so you know, I may look younger than I am now, but it won't be that way forever.'"

Kenna smiled wide and nodded slowly.

"That sounds like Cooper. I doona think there is need for Rosie to apologize come morning. I verra much doubt that Rosie's words wounded him at all."

If Kenna was correct, the boy was indeed much more grown-up than he appeared. Malcolm knew that at such an age, to be called small by a girl he liked would've been crushing.

"She will apologize whether Cooper needs the apology or not. No matter how upset Rosie is at her own situation, it gives her no right to intentionally try to hurt others."

Kenna resumed picking at the edges around the pie.

"Aye, fine. 'Tis o'course yer choice what ye have her do. I only meant that I doona want ye to worry for Cooper's feelings. His whole life he's dealt with people underestimating him, and he always handles it with grace. He's been a grown man trapped inside a child's body since the day I first met him."

Setting her fork to the side, Kenna pushed the pie toward him and Malcolm stood to clean up the table.

Discarding the few scraps that remained and placing the dish in the sink to wash later, Malcolm returned to his seat.

"I've no doubt of that. Since the day you met him?"

"Aye. Cooper is not my grandson by birth, though I love him no differently than those who are. His mother married my son only a few years ago."

"Ah. And how do you know Morna and Jerry? Cooper seems quite close with them."

Malcolm watched as Kenna hesitated a long moment and he couldn't help but wonder what about the question gave her pause.

"She's a distant relative of mine through marriage. My husband was her cousin. Morna and Cooper took to one another the moment they met. I suppose she and Jerry are in some way grandparents to him, as well, now. The child has many."

"He is blessed then. I'm the only grandparent Rosie has left."

The confession slipped from Malcolm without thought, and he immediately felt strange. He hated nothing more than other people's sympathy, and it took much for him to open up. Why then, had he spoken so easily of something so delicate with this stranger?

Thankfully, Kenna gave little in the way of sympathy.

"'Tis always difficult when children lose those they love at a young age. Is yer wife recently passed? Is that what wounds the girl now?"

Malcolm looked into Kenna's eyes and saw no pity. She didn't avoid his gaze, didn't smile softly to make him comfortable. It endeared her to him even more. And somehow, it made it easier to speak of things he rarely ever did.

"No. Rosie is named after her grandmother though she never knew her. My Rosalind has been gone seventeen years now. Rosie's father passed away two years ago this next week, and while she still grieves for him, her anger is now directed at her mother.

She was supposed to be on this trip with us. She claims she is swamped with work, but Rosie knows better. I don't blame her for her anger. I'm angry, as well. She does not, however, have reason to make everyone else around her—most especially strangers—miserable."

"Not a one of us is miserable, Mac. Allow the girl her anger. She will come around in a few days. If I know Morna, she will see to it that Rosie's mood lifts sooner rather than later. Now," Kenna stood and stretched just slightly before turning away from him, "while I can scarcely believe it myself, I feel as if I could sleep even more. Thank ye for the food. I should go back to bed."

"You're very welcome. Sleep well." He hesitated to do so as she climbed the stairs, but couldn't keep from calling out to her once more as she reached the top. "Kenna?"

She turned toward him with a smile. "Aye?"

"Thank you."

"For what?"

"I didn't leave that conversation feeling sorry for Rosie or myself. I don't remember the last time I felt that way after speaking to anyone about our losses."

Her voice was quiet, but her tone was sad as she answered him.

"Doona thank me. My lack of sympathy wasna intentional, I assure ye. Perhaps my own dealings with grief have hardened me more than I knew. Goodnight, Mac. Rosie is lucky to have ye."

As Malcolm waited for her bedroom door to close, he knew he wouldn't sleep a wink tonight for wondering about what had pained his beautiful new friend so much.

espite my insistence that I was indeed still sleepy after my many hours long nap, I didn't sleep a minute after returning to my room. Instead, I lay awake thinking of Malcolm— of how easy it was to speak to him, of how polite he'd been not to mention my appearance earlier in the night, of how handsome he looked dressed so casually for sleep. It was the first time in well over a decade that such thoughts of a man had occupied my mind.

Eventually, just past five when I knew Cooper would be awake. I tiptoed over to his room and slipped inside.

As expected, he sat propped up in his bed with a mound of pillows, a book on his lap. He lay his book down beside him and smiled at me as I entered.

"What are you doing up so early, Nana?"

"'Twas the nap I took last evening. I slept far longer than I should have. Cooper, I'm sorry for not tending to ye last night. I quite abandoned ye."

He shook his head and scooted over so I could sit down beside him.

"You didn't abandon me. I'm used to being with Morna and

Jerry all by myself. I didn't think anything about it, I promise. Do you feel more rested?"

I suspected my sleeping patterns would be turned around for days, but for now, I did feel quite rested.

"Aye, I do. What of ye, Cooper, did ye sleep well?"

Gently laying his head against my shoulder, Cooper answered.

"Yes. I always sleep well. Maybe it's 'cause I know Morna has magic, but I always feel completely safe here. I don't worry about anything."

"Do ye not usually feel safe at home?"

"I do, but magic just sort of brings a whole other level of safety to it, ya know?"

I laughed and gently rested my own head against the top of his.

"Aye, I suppose ye are right. Cooper, Malcolm came to see me last night. He wished to apologize on behalf of Rosie."

The child lifted his head and twisted to face me. His brows pulled toward his nose in confusion.

"What for?"

"He was worried that she might have wounded yer feelings over dinner."

Cooper smiled widely. While the light was low in the room, I thought I saw a slight blush in his cheeks.

"She didn't hurt my feelings."

"No? What she said to ye wasna verra kind."

"No it wasn't, but she's not really upset with me. I know that. I think she's *wonderful.*"

I had to swallow the giggle that rose up in my throat at the sound of complete awe in Cooper's voice as he called Rosie wonderful. It seemed that Malcolm was right—Cooper fancied the lass.

"Wonderful...how so?"

Cooper hesitated and crossed his arms as he pursed his lips.

"I wish I had a better answer, but the truth is, I just don't know her that well yet. It's just a feeling I have. Rosie is something special. Don't worry though—I'll get to know her. She may not think much of me now, but someday I'll grow. Then she will like me so much, it will drive her crazy."

The thought seemed to delight Cooper.

"So ye think ye will know Rosalind for a long time, then? Ye doona believe that once she and her grandfather leave that ye willna see her again?"

Cooper smiled and turned his head to look up under his lashes at me with an expression that was meant to tell me that I should've already known the answer.

"Nana, don't you know how Morna works by now? She hasn't admitted it yet, even though I tried to get her to, but I know Morna's magic has something to do with them being here. I have no doubt that Mac and Rosie will be in our lives for a very long time. Do you doubt it, Nana?"

It truly hadn't crossed my mind until now. Everything about the situation seemed entirely coincidental, but perhaps Cooper was right. If he was, did her plans only relate to Cooper and Rosie, or did it all have something to do with me and Mac, as well?

"*I* see that ye did find yer way to the kitchen after the rest of us were abed. I'm glad for it, lass. It dinna please me to go to bed without seeing ye fed, but I dinna wish to wake ye, either. Did Mac help ye heat everything?"

Entering the kitchen after my first glorious experience with a shower, I moved to where Morna worked over a flame to see what she was cooking.

"Aye, he did. Do ye need help with anything?"

Morna quickly waved me away.

"No, lass. 'Tis only eggs, and the toast and coffee are nearly ready. I've also some haggis and black pudding for ye and Jerry. No one else will eat it."

"Not even ye?" Morna was as Scottish as I. It surprised me that she would dislike food she'd undoubtedly been raised on.

"No, I've not touched either food since the age of ten when I learned what each item was made of. If my brother or father were still here, they'd think it traitorous of me to say so, but I canna stomach it."

I'd never given the making of either food much thought. I had no intention of doing so now. Eager to change the subject, I quickly peeked inside the living room to make certain that Malcolm still slept soundly on the floor.

With his soft snores audible from the bottom of the stairway, I knew it was safe to ask my question.

"Morna, how do ye and Jerry know Malcolm and Rosalind?"

Extending a mug in my direction, Morna carried her own over to the small table and motioned for me to sit next to her.

"Well, we dinna know Rosalind until last night, and it has been many a year since we've seen Malcolm. As for how we know him, in truth, 'tis his brother, Kraig, that we knew first. We met Kraig at the hospital in Edinburgh when Jerry had his knee replaced over a decade ago. He was his surgeon, and despite Jerry being the most cantankerous patient the poor doctor ever had, the two of them took to each other. We've been friends with the young lad ever since. In fact, I introduced Kraig to his wife, Emilia. We met Malcolm at their wedding."

Smiling, I shook my head.

"It shouldna surprise me to hear that, Morna, but for some reason, it does. Have ye ever met a singleton whose love life ye havena decided to meddle in?"

I knew the moment I saw her mischievous grin what I'd walked into.

"Ye are still single, Kenna. I've yet to meddle in yer life."

"Cooper is none too sure of that. He told me this morning he believes Malcolm and Rosie's appearance here is yer doing. And I'm not certain that being widowed is the same as being single."

Morna laughed and reached over to pat my hand.

"Mayhap for the first few years after such a loss, such an answer is acceptable. While ye are widowed, ye are free to love again. It has been fifteen years, Kenna. Ye are verra, verra single."

"So..." I took a sip of my coffee to listen for Malcolm's snoring. It still reverberated through the hallway. "Is Cooper right, Morna? Have ye decided to meddle in my life next?"

Morna scooted her chair right next to mine and leaned in to whisper.

"Believe it or not, lass, my magic is not the only force in this world which conspires to bring those that are meant to be together, together. While I know Cooper dinna believe me, I had no hand in this. I canna begin to tell ye how surprised I was when I saw Jerry pull up with two extra guests."

I leaned away from her. "Why are ye whispering, Morna?"

Grinning, she leaned in even closer and kept her voice low.

"Kenna, Mac has been feigning sleep since ye came down those stairs. There is no need for him to hear what I'm telling ye. Now, while I promise ye I had nothing to do with ye all finding Rosie yesterday, that doesna mean that there is no reason for his arrival. The two of ye would make a fair match, 'tis plain to see. And while I'll not use magic in this instance, I would be lying if I said I had no intention of meddling. I intend to clear the path for the two of ye just a bit, just to allow ye to see where things might lead. I would advise ye not to get in my way."

Before I could protest or even respond, Morna stood, winked at me, and then screamed out for everyone in the house to hear, "Breakfast is ready. All of ye best wake and come to the kitchen before it cools."

CHAPTER 9

By mid-morning, Morna began to execute her "light meddling." Over breakfast she all but begged Malcolm and Rosalind to stay one more day so they could help us decorate the inn for Christmas. With Rosie quite reluctant to return to Edinburgh, Malcolm agreed.

With Morna, Jerry, Cooper, and Rosie pulling down boxes from the attic, the nosy and insistent witch sent Malcolm and me out on a task to find the perfect Christmas tree from a farm a half hour away.

Knowing that Morna believed us to be a good match changed the dynamic between us. While Malcolm hadn't been able to hear our conversation, it had shifted something in my own mind, which made me nervous and awkward in his presence. I couldn't look at him without wondering "what if?", without thinking through a thousand different scenarios, without questioning whether or not my feelings were a result of actually liking him or simply the result of being on my own for so many years. Back home, I'd quickly ended any possibility of a relationship with anyone else—I'd never been interested in the slightest. Now, for some reason completely beyond me, I was.

Was it the trip? Had being away from home and in a time so unfamiliar simply overexcited me so much that I was seeing possibility, that I was seeing attraction, where it wasn't? I found this the most likely cause of my feelings and did my best to silence the endless chatter of thoughts in my mind as we pulled away from the inn.

"Don't you find it odd that the kids didn't want to come pick out a tree?"

Laughing, I remembered both children's faces when they'd told us that they wanted to stay and help Morna and Jerry get the decorations down. It was evident in their glee that Morna had somehow offered them something that appealed to them even more.

"I suspect we will return to find both of them so sick from whatever sweet treats Morna has bribed them with that 'twill be clear why they wished to stay."

"Why would she bribe them?" Malcolm's tone was genuinely curious, and I realized once more that he truly hadn't been able to hear Morna's whisperings to me.

A younger woman would've lied—would've made some excuse that kept awkwardness at bay—but sometime during my forties, my worries over what others thought of me had blessedly diminished. Being relieved of that torture was entirely worth the cost of the wrinkles such a decade had brought me. If this man was meant to like me, he would. If not, he wouldn't. Bringing up Morna's thoughts on the matter wouldn't change things one way or the other.

"Morna sent us on this errand so that we would be alone. She believes we would make a good couple."

I expected him to make light of such a statement. He did anything but.

"Does she? Well, I don't know you well enough yet to know if she's right, but I'll not go so far as to disagree with the old woman either. She said the same of my brother once, and she couldn't have been more right."

His use of the word *yet* warmed me from naval to nose. I could fool no one. While I might not care what the average stranger thought, I very much wanted this man to like me. For with each new thing he said, I found myself liking him just a little bit more.

---

*L*ord only knew how they would get the tree Kenna picked back to Morna and Jerry's. The car was small, the tree large, but Malcolm couldn't find it in himself to deny her. She was right anyway—the tree was perfect. It would fill the window in Morna and Jerry's inn, and once it was lit and decorated, it would be visible from the road to all who passed by.

"I can tell by the way ye are staring at it, ye doona think we can get it back. 'Tis fine, Mac. While this one is beautiful, I doona mind if we find one a bit smaller. No one else will mind, either."

"No, no." He reached out and placed his hand on her back to reassure her. "They will help get it situated on top of the car. We have plenty of straps to get it secured. I just...you may have to help direct me when turning corners and such. I suspect it will hang down a bit over the windshield. It's going to block part of my view."

"Oh. Well, aye, I can certainly try to do so."

"Great. Let's go pay for it."

They walked side by side to the station where they could pay for the tree and await some assistance. As they passed the car, Kenna stepped away and called back to him.

"I'll meet ye there. I left the money Morna gave us in the car."

"No need. The least I can do for her allowing Rosie and me to stay is buy them a tree. I'll pay for it myself, and I'll leave the extra money with Jerry, for I know Morna won't take it back if I try to give it to her."

Malcolm waited for Kenna to return to his side before approaching the young woman taking payment for the trees.

As he reached into his wallet for his credit card, Kenna leaned into him, her voice shy.

"What is that?"

He didn't have any idea what she referred to.

"What is what?"

She pointed to the card in his hand, and he struggled to keep confusion from etching his face.

"Oh, it's my credit card. I spent the last of my pounds at the Conall Castle gift shop. I need to find another ATM once Rosie and I return to Edinburgh. I doubt there's another one close."

Kenna continued to look at the square piece of plastic quizzically.

"'Tis money?"

He nodded and slowly handed the card to the young woman in front of them who unabashedly looked at Kenna with the confusion he was trying so hard to hide.

"Yes. In a sense. Don't you have one?"

Kenna shook her head. Malcolm had visited Scotland many, many times. The entire country was entirely modernized. Even isles that only had access to larger stores if they traveled by ferry had their own small shops that accepted credit cards. How did anyone in today's society not know what a credit card was?

"Kenna, what part of Scotland did you say you were from?"

Malcolm watched as her face changed, shielding her curiosity as she righted herself and smiled at him.

"I dinna say. Doona worry. I can see well enough what it does. I believe I'll wait in the car."

He didn't know if he'd ever been so baffled in his life. Clearly, while Kenna could see that the card had served its purpose to pay for the tree, she had no idea how it worked. And her quick dismissal of her curiosity once she realized he found it odd confused him even more.

Something was strange about this woman. He very much wanted to find out what it was.

CHAPTER 10

he ease with which I was able to speak with Malcolm had lowered my guard. I was accustomed to being around twenty-first century people who knew precisely from which time I came and had no problem explaining to me all the things I didn't know. What had happened with Malcolm was exactly what I'd feared most when Mitsy had suggested such a trip. I looked like a fool, and I couldn't begin to tell him why.

I said nothing on the ride back to Morna's, save for the occasional direction I would give by leaning my head out of the car window to make sure that the road was clear. Thankfully, Malcolm said nothing of the incident at the Christmas tree farm. For the second time of me embarrassing myself in front of him, he proved himself to be a gentleman. There was at least some comfort in that.

When we returned to the inn, everyone was delighted at our choice of tree, as I knew they would be. The boxes of decorations were down, and everything was dusted and laid out for us to decorate.

We all had a wonderful time, and as the day went on and Malcolm didn't treat me like a mad woman, my worry abated. We all visited, laughed, decorated, and drank more than our fair share of hot chocolate as we worked together to make Morna and Jerry's home one of the most splendidly beautiful Christmas homes I'd ever seen.

By the time night fell, we were all exhausted and happy.

"It has been some years since Jerry and I had the energy to place so many lovely decorations out ourselves. Most years we just settle for a simple tree and a few strands of lights. This year's display makes my heart happier than any of ye can know. Thank ye for yer help. Now, let us sit down and enjoy one last meal together before Mac and Rosie leave us for Edinburgh tomorrow."

I'd known they were leaving. They weren't even supposed to be here today, but somehow through the day's festivities I'd forgotten, and the reminder that our new friends would be gone saddened me more than I wished to admit.

What would I do for the next two weeks without Malcolm here? While I'd never expected to meet him, suddenly the next days at the inn with only Cooper, Morna, and Jerry to occupy me, left me feeling rather empty.

It seemed that I wasn't the only one with such emotion, for over dinner, few words were exchanged—not until dessert was being finished and a hesitant Rosie glanced over at Morna for courage before addressing her grandfather.

"Pops, I have a question for you."

We all watched on as Malcolm lay his fork on his plate and looked over at Rosalind.

"You do? What is it?"

"Do we have to go back to Edinburgh? We always do the same things there. You visit with Uncle Kraig and Aunt Emilia, and I get stuck playing solitaire. Then you guys drag me around to fancy restaurants I don't even like until the real fun begins on Christmas Eve. Can't we stay here until then and then go back to Edinburgh in time for actual Christmas?"

If that was indeed what the young girl's Christmases in Edinburgh looked like, I didn't blame her at all for wanting to stay with Morna. Hope fluttered inside me as I watched Mac contemplate Rosie's plea.

"There's part of me that wishes we could, but I have tickets to the symphony tomorrow night. They were expensive and difficult to get. Plus, Kraig and Emilia would be very disappointed. I'm sorry, Rosie. We need to go back tomorrow."

"I have an idea."

Horrified, I looked over at Cooper and shook my head as I tried to stop him.

"No, Coop. We doona intrude on other people's business. Malcolm has given his answer. Ye doona need to suggest any ideas."

While not normally one to disobey, Cooper unabashedly argued with me.

"Why not? It's a good idea. I think Malcolm would like to hear it."

Just as I meant to speak more harshly to him, Malcolm stepped in to rescue Cooper.

"It's okay, Kenna. What's your idea, Cooper?"

Now that he was allowed to speak, Cooper hesitated.

"What...what if Rosie stayed here and you went to Edinburgh with Nana? I know she would like to see the city at Christmastime, and I doubt that we would make the trip there on our own. She's more likely to enjoy the stuff that Rosie wouldn't."

Before I had a moment to object or Malcolm had a moment to answer, Morna smiled and stood from the table as she started to gather dishes.

"Why Cooper, 'tis a splendid idea. Malcolm, ye know we would take great care of Rosie. The lassie expressed a desire to learn how to bake this afternoon while ye and Kenna were away. If I had a few days with her, I could teach her much."

Rosie quickly chimed in, her voice filled with anticipation.

"Oh, please let me, Pops. This school break has been rotten so far. If Mom's not going to be here for Christmas, you could at least let me do something I want to do for a few days. Please let me stay. Go and do the things you have to do in Edinburgh and then come back and get me in a few days. Please. I would love you forever, Pops, if you'd let me."

I saw the exact moment Malcolm surrendered. Smiling, he nodded.

"Okay, okay. Fine. If you want to stay here a few days, that's fine, Rosie. I have no doubt you'd have more fun here with Cooper than you would in Edinburgh. But you've all made quite the assumption by assuming that Kenna would even want to accompany me."

Speaking with as much enthusiasm as the children, I interrupted him as Grace's insistence that I not concern myself with Cooper while here crossed my mind.

"I do want to. I really, really do."

There was an excitement in Malcolm's eyes as he looked at me that caused the hairs on the back of my neck to stand on end.

"I'm pleased to hear it. We'll leave first thing in the morning."

CHAPTER 11

$\mathcal{T}$he drive to Edinburgh the following morning in the car Morna had "delivered" for us during the night, was long, but nowhere near the length of time it would've taken me to travel there in my own time. I was in a constant state of amazement in this century, but I promised myself before leaving the inn with Malcolm that I would not make the same mistake I'd made the day before. If something confused or surprised me, I would keep my reaction to myself and make a special note to ask Cooper about whatever I saw once I returned to get him in three days' time.

Pulling into the city required me to stifle all sorts of emotions. While Edinburgh's grand castle still sat on top of the city center, so much else had changed. The lights, the cars, the noise—I wasn't sure I was a good enough actress to hide my utter amazement.

"I called my brother last night after everything was decided. They're expecting you. No need to be nervous."

Perhaps that's how my excitement looked to him with the way I was all but bouncing in my seat with my eyes peeled outside the window, but in truth, I wasn't nervous at all. I was delighted at the opportunity to explore this time period. While I'd listened to everyone's insistence that I enjoy this time and see as much as I could while here, I'd not really expected such an opportunity to arise.

The city was beautiful at Christmas—covered in snow, with garland and lights strung up over many buildings and doorways.

I didn't realize I'd not replied to him until Malcolm spoke up again.

"Are you all right, Kenna? You've hardly said anything since we left Morna and Jerry's."

Reluctant to look away from the window on the chance that I might miss something wonderful, I turned my head and smiled at him. He was right—I'd been quite rude.

"Ach, I'm sorry, Malcolm. 'Tis only that I canna remember the last time I was so excited about anything. I've simply been enjoying the view."

He smiled a crooked smile, and my heart sped up in response. The view outside was wonderful, but I couldn't have been missing anything that looked better than looking at him.

"You don't get to Edinburgh very often, then?"

I answered honestly. "The last time I was in Edinburgh, I was fifteen years old."

He looked as if he didn't believe me.

"Truly? Have you lived in Scotland all your life, or did you leave here for a while?"

"Aye, and all of my life."

Malcolm slowed the car and turned the corner onto a street lined with tall, connected buildings with doorways lining the front and steps leading up to each one. They looked like homes, though I'd never known homes to be connected in such a way.

"In what part of Scotland do you live, Kenna? I still haven't gotten an answer from you."

I wasn't sure how to answer him. I didn't know just how familiar he was with Scotland's geography. If he was familiar at all, it wouldn't be difficult for him to catch me in a lie. Most especially since I had no way of knowing if areas that were once remote, still were today. I decided it best to lie as little as possible.

"I live with my...my nephew at McMillan Castle. McMillan is my last name. He and his wife run the castle and keep it open to visitors. I assist in managing the staff."

It was an answer that was only about halfway true, but I saw no way for him to be able to discern that I lied.

His face lit up, as if my words had suddenly solved a great mystery.

"Ah! Well, that explains it, then. I'm sure you have people that bring whatever you need to the castle. If so, there wouldn't be much need for you to leave the area or to do your own shopping."

While I didn't quite appreciate the insinuation that others did everything for me, I couldn't argue the point. In truth, there was much that was taken care of for me. I was a remarkably blessed woman in any century.

Slightly embarrassed, I nodded.

"Aye. Though 'tis not as if I couldna do any of those things myself if I needed to."

His hand reached across the space between us and squeezed my hand as the car slowed to a stop in front of one of the doorways.

"I wasn't suggesting that you couldn't. That just explains your reaction to my credit card at the Christmas tree farm yesterday. Hey, McMillan Castle is the one with all of the extraordinary Christmas decorations, isn't it? Rosie has wanted to see it for years. Perhaps, you could arrange a special tour for us?"

I nodded and then pointed to the woman who had just appeared in the doorway closest to the car.

"Aye. O'course I can. Is that Emilia?"

I knew her name from Rosie's mention of them yesterday. The

moment a man cradling a baby appeared next to her, I knew I was right.

"Yes, it is. She will be thrilled to meet you. Don't worry about your bag. I'll get them after we say hello."

The moment I stepped outside the car, the woman called to me.

"Kenna, lass, if ye wish to see Edinburgh at Christmas, ye have come to the right place. While he may not be Scottish himself, Malcolm knows the city better than even I do. 'Tis a shame, but it seems that it often happens in such a way. Locals doona appreciate the uniqueness of a city the same way that visitors do, so we doona get out and see as much."

Emilia talked quickly and without end as she wrapped one arm around my shoulder and led me inside their home.

While quite small, the home was beautiful and welcoming. I'd been unable to keep up with Emilia's chattering. Just as I worried that I wouldn't be able to answer her should she ask me a question, I was rescued by a hand at my back and turned to greet Malcolm's brother.

The man, while shorter than Malcolm, still stood far above the top of my head. He strongly resembled his brother with the same thick dark hair and brows. But where Malcolm had blue eyes, Kraig had brown, and his face was clean-shaven. He also had no gray in his hair. As I examined his face, I looked over his smooth unweathered skin and saw a man not much older than my sons. Kraig Warren looked all of twenty years younger than his elder brother.

"Welcome to Edinburgh. You must be Rosie's new favorite person. By agreeing to come with Malcolm, she got to stay away. I know we were boring her to tears."

Kraig pulled me in tight with one arm while still holding the baby in his other arm. Once he released me, I reached out and placed my palm gently on top of the babe's head.

"And this must be Robbie, aye?"

Kraig nodded, and the glimmer in his eyes as he looked at his son nearly brought tears to my eyes.

"Yes. I don't imagine he will sleep too much longer, though. Soon he will bid you a proper hello by screaming at the top of his lungs."

I grinned as he walked away and Malcolm came up behind me. He must've read my mind for he leaned in close to answer the question I'd not yet asked him.

"Kraig was the surprise of my mother's life. She had him when I was twenty-eight years old, at the age of forty-four. Our father was forty-eight. My mother and my wife were pregnant at the same time." He laughed. "It was a very strange time in my life."

Eyes wide, I looked up at him.

"Ach, God bless her. Kraig would've been seven years old when yer mother was my age. I canna imagine it. My grandchildren are work enough. Did she..." I hesitated. "Did she live long enough to raise him?"

Malcolm smiled and pointed to a photo on the small table to my left.

"Oh, yes. She's still very much alive. You'd never guess she's as old as she is. She lives in Scotland now, just across the street actually. I'm sure you will meet her either tonight or tomorrow." He paused and his brows pulled in. "Which I suppose means that I lied to you before, though I didn't mean to. My mother is technically a grandparent to Rosie, but she's lived in Scotland since Rosie was born. They're not very close."

I'd thought nothing of it.

"It takes more than blood to form a bond, Malcolm. Look at wee Cooper. I am not his blood, but I am no less his grandmother for it. In the same way, blood doesna necessarily make someone a grandparent. Ye dinna lie."

"Oh look at the two of ye. Look where ye are standing."

Emilia stood in the kitchen but pointed to us. She looked thrilled. We both looked blankly back at her.

"Ye are under the mistletoe. Come now, Malcolm. Ye must kiss her. 'Tis bad luck if ye doona do so."

I'd not been kissed in fifteen years. My entire body seized up with nerves at the thought of being kissed now. Surely, I'd forgotten how. Surely, I would do it all wrong.

I had little time to think on it as Malcolm's hand slipped to my lower back and he pulled me gently against him, his head quickly bending to my ear.

"You heard her. We can't have bad luck following you around."

I'd always thought the notion of women swooning in response to a man's touch lacking in realism. I was a level-headed woman— ahead of my time is what my daughters-in-law always called me— but as Malcolm's lips brushed against my own, I knew that if not for his steady hand holding me tight, I would've dropped to the floor like a sack of flour.

It was that wonderfully, deliciously good.

CHAPTER 12

"*A*re you awake? I was surprised to see the fire still burning when I woke to relieve Emilia for a little while."

Malcolm stood from his makeshift bed on the couch and waved his brother downstairs to join him.

"Yes, wide awake. Here, why don't you hand me Robbie. I'll bounce him until he goes back to sleep. You can go back to bed if you wish."

While his brother didn't hesitate to hand him the baby, he didn't turn around and head back upstairs.

"I'm awake now, too. I'll stay up and visit with you. I haven't had a chance to visit with you alone yet."

Malcolm knew well enough what his brother would ask him, and he had no answers to give him.

Whether it was the touch of someone new or just the fact that Malcolm was so warm from laying near the fire, young Robbie relaxed instantly as Malcolm cradled him in his arms. He continued to bounce the child gently as he walked around the room.

"It's been a long time since I've held a baby—not since Rosie was one."

Kicking Malcolm's pillow onto the floor, his brother collapsed onto the couch and propped his feet up on the coffee table.

"You've always been good with them, but I don't want to talk to you about babies."

Keeping his voice low so Robbie would continue to drift to sleep, Malcolm walked over behind the couch.

"I know what you want to talk about, but there's not anything for me to say."

"Sure there is. You didn't tell me anything on the phone yesterday when you called to tell me she was coming with you. Who is she?"

Malcolm still knew so little about her. Just as he'd begun to believe that her strange behavior at the Christmas tree farm had been explained away, her behavior at the symphony had raised new questions in his mind.

He couldn't recall a single melody the symphony played. He'd spent the entire two hours watching her take in the spectacle.

She looked on with the wonder of a small child. As the lights changed around the stage, her eyes darted around to watch them as if looking for the source. When the conductor stepped up to the microphone and his voice boomed out over the audience, she'd nearly fallen out of her chair. It was the strangest thing he'd ever seen. It was incredibly enchanting. Wonder was something he'd not felt in decades. That Kenna could still be so surprised and fascinated by anything at their age was one of her many attractive qualities, but it still made no sense.

"I've only known her a few days. She's related to Morna and Jerry. She and her grandson were visiting them when Rosie and I intruded on their trip. The rest is exactly what you've heard. Rosie wanted to stay and Kenna wanted to see Edinburgh at Christmas. So here we are."

His brother twisted in his seat on the couch and looked back at him.

"And that's it then. She's just your friend?"

Kenna had given him no indication that she was interested in anything more than his friendship. While he hoped that would change, he couldn't claim that they were more than that now.

He nodded and his brother stood from the chair and reached for Robbie as he shook his head.

"I wonder what Emilia would say if I kissed one of my female friends under the mistletoe like that? I can't imagine that she would be very pleased."

I woke sometime in the early hours of the morning, just past midnight, with my bladder so full I thought it might burst. While I knew it probable that there was a restroom somewhere on the top floor, I had no desire to start opening doors in the dark, and I knew with certainty that there was one just past the front door on the bottom floor.

With Malcolm sleeping on the living room couch, I opened the bedroom door quietly, intending to sneak through the house unnoticed. Instead, as I opened it, I could hear voices from down below, and the staircase was illuminated by the fire that still burned.

"And that's it then. She's just your friend?"

It was Kraig's voice. I knew I should back up into the room and close the door and hold it until morning—Malcolm's answer to his brother's question was not something he intended me to hear, but I desperately wanted to know his answer. Instead, I moved just a little closer to the staircase and listened.

Nothing. Malcolm gave no answer. Before I could move away, Kraig was moving toward the staircase with the baby in his arms, calling back over his shoulder something about kissing his friends under the mistletoe.

Knowing that I could do nothing to keep from being seen, I spoke out to try and avoid the uncomfortable interaction that was headed my way.

"Kraig, is the baby awake? I was just going down to the restroom but if ye'd like me to take him for ye, I'd be happy to."

Kraig smiled at me and reached a hand out to gently squeeze my arm in thanks.

"No need now. Malcolm got him to sleep. I hope we didn't wake you."

Perhaps too dramatically, I dismissed him with a wave of my hand.

"No, ye dinna at all. I dinna even know ye were down here until I saw ye coming toward me on the stairs. Goodnight, Kraig."

Hopeful that I'd covered up my eavesdropping well enough, I made my way downstairs to where Malcolm stood behind the couch.

"Ye should be asleep, Mac. Ye promised me a full day of sightseeing tomorrow, and I'll not let ye out of it even if ye are tired."

He laughed and looked down at me. I suddenly felt very self-conscious in Adelle's robe.

"I think my anticipation for tomorrow is precisely why I can't sleep. Don't worry. I won't back out on you."

Leaving him to return to bed, I went to the restroom and came out with every intention of sneaking back upstairs. Instead, I walked past the living room to find Malcolm sitting on the couch as he faced the fire.

"Do ye not wish to at least attempt some sleep?"

Using his head to wave me over, he didn't face me as he spoke.

"Why don't you come and sit by me a minute? Maybe after some conversation, I'll feel like sleeping."

I knew he'd not meant anything unkind, but I didn't hesitate to point out what his words had suggested.

"Well, thank ye. I'm so pleased to hear that speaking with me is an effective way to put ye to sleep."

He laughed, his voice deep. Knowing that I would now sleep little myself, I went to join him. He sat at one end of the couch with both the middle and its other end unoccupied. I began to retreat to the couch's other end, but the warmth of him was too alluring. Cautiously, I slid closer toward the middle.

"You know I didn't mean it that way. Kenna..." he hesitated as I turned to look at him. The glow from the fire made his eyes look even more blue than usual. With the memory of his lips against mine still fresh in my mind, I couldn't keep my eyes from drifting toward his mouth.

"Aye?"

"May I ask you a question?"

"Ye may."

He reached for my hands. I adored how strong and warm his grip was. His hands completely enveloped my own.

"What are we doing? I'm past the age where games suit me. Shall we be friends or is it possible that we might be something more?"

I could hear my heart beating in my ears. There was only one thing I wanted to do in answer to his question.

With my hands still clasped in his, I closed the space between us and leaned in to kiss him.

The urging of all the twenty-first century women in my life sounding in my mind, I allowed myself to stop thinking as I moved against him, opening to his tongue as his hands pulled away and moved to the sides of my face. We kissed until my body shook all over from need. Recognizing where this would lead if I didn't stop soon, I pulled away.

"Was that your answer? If so, I'm very much in agreement with it."

71

Malcolm's own breath was shaky, and the need in his eyes made it difficult for me to breathe. I scooted away to give myself the space to gather my composure.

"In a way, though 'twas not all of my answer. I wish to tell ye something."

While I was here, I wanted Malcolm. I wanted to feel alive, to dust off some of the neglected parts of my soul and body, but I needed him to understand that I could promise nothing beyond the next few days. It wouldn't be fair to either of us to enter into something that was bound to cause us eventual pain without knowing exactly what would come.

"Tell me. I would listen to you say anything."

Hesitantly, my voice unsteady as the effects of his kiss continued to course through me, I told him everything that was on my mind.

"Mac, I was fourteen when I married my husband—still a child. And while I did love him in my own way—I never would've chosen him for myself. He was two verra different people, and I kept my distance from him because of it. He was a remarkable father to his children—fair and gentle with them all his life. But William was far too serious and harsh with me. He never laughed when we were together, and I only saw him smile in the presence of his sons. Our marriage cost me much of my childhood, but for him, our marriage cost him the woman he truly wanted to marry. While I played no hand in our betrothal, I doona think he ever forgave me for it."

I could see the question in Malcolm's eyes and paused to give him time to ask it.

"It was an arranged marriage? At fourteen? That's outrageous, Kenna."

Ignoring most of his questions, I continued.

"Aye, 'twas arranged from the time of my birth. If there is a blessing to come from it, 'tis that William vowed to never force his own children into such an agreement. Despite our lack of passion for one another, we lived easily together as husband and wife.

"William has been gone for fifteen years now, and there's been no one since then. I only tell ye this so that ye may understand why I'm about to propose something that may not be acceptable to ye. If 'tis not, I willna blame ye for it."

I waited for him to say something, but instead he just nodded, urging me onward.

"I've never known what 'tis like to explore a relationship of my wanting. If I were wiser, I would stifle what I feel for ye now and accept yer friendship. But Malcolm, for once in my life, I wish to be selfish. I wish to be selfish even knowing that in a few days, we will go back to Morna and Jerry's where ye will collect Rosie and I will most likely never see ye again. We live in verra different worlds, we canna pretend otherwise. So..." I was shaking all over again, but no longer from need. I'd never felt so vulnerable, so open to rejection. "To answer yer question after a verra long explanation—aye—I wish to be more than friends with ye, but I canna promise ye that anything shall last past the next few days. Can ye accept that and not think me the most selfish of women?"

Malcolm looked at me for a long moment, the need still evident in his gaze. He smiled slowly. As he pulled me against him, he whispered in my ear.

"Kenna, I will take you any way I can get you for as long as you'll allow me. I've never been one to worry too much about the future. All we have is now."

As his lips began to nip at the length of my neck, I allowed myself to drown in the sensation of his touch, quickly silencing the small voice in my mind that insisted I'd just asked him to agree to something I would never be able to uphold myself.

CHAPTER 13

*M*alcolm stayed true to his promise. Despite the fact that we both were sleep deprived after spending most of the night visiting, cuddling, and aye, occasionally kissing by the fire, he was up and ready for our day in the city before I was.

I found twenty-first century clothing so much more difficult to assemble. In my own time, I owned only four dresses save for the two I reserved for only the most special of occasions. There was nothing to think about when getting dressed—no decisions to make and no make-up to fuss with. With the assortment of items Adelle packed for me, I was left confused each and every morning as I tried to piece together items of clothing that would look nice together.

Since it was freezing outside and snowing on and off almost every day, I chose a pair of tight jeans, boots that went over them almost up to my knee, and a thick wine-colored sweater. After throwing on a hat, a scarf, some gloves, and my coat, I was ready to go.

I was determined not to apologize for making him wait on me.

It was known across all time periods and countries that women take longer.

"So, what do ye have planned for the day?"

Seeing that I was already bundled up for outside, Malcolm reached for his own coat and scarf, donning them as he spoke to me.

"Lots. I'll drive us closer to the city center. Then I thought we could get a ticket for the double-decker buses. I'm sure being Scottish, you'll find them very touristy, but they really aren't a bad way to get from place to place, and it helps you get a layout of the whole city."

I was only familiar with the word *bus* because of the bus Malcolm and Rosie had been on at Conall Castle. I hadn't the slightest idea what a double-decker bus could be.

"I will find nothing too touristy, Mac, I assure ye. I've never been on a double-decker bus."

Surprise framed his features. It was an expression he wore often around me, and try as I might to not give away how out of sorts I was in this time, it was impossible to always say just the right thing.

"Well, good. Then you won't mind it. Here's a summary of the itinerary I have planned for us. If there's anything you don't want to do, just tell me, and we'll find something else."

When I nodded, he looked down at his list and began to read.

"First, after taking the whole bus loop, I thought we could grab breakfast at Emilia's favorite café. She used to work there as a teenager. They have the best coffee in Edinburgh."

I smiled as I glanced over to see Emilia nodding enthusiastically.

"Sounds perfect."

"Next, I thought we would go over to the German Christmas Market. They have some of the prettiest trinkets and toys you've ever seen, and there's a big ferris wheel that will give us a spectacular view of the city."

Again, I had no idea what a ferris wheel was, but I said nothing.

"Afterwards, I thought we could go to The Dome for lunch in the tea room and to see their unbelievable decorations."

He paused and looked up at me and I knew he was wanting some sort of confirmation that all his plans were okay with me.

"I canna wait, Malcolm."

He let out a big breath of relief and grinned with pride as he looked back down at the list. The gesture made him look two decades younger—slightly nervous and even a little shy.

"Okay, after lunch, I thought we could explore the Scottish Market for a bit and then go on a tour of Edinburgh Castle."

"Oh, aye, let's. I would love to see the castle." Edinburgh Castle was the one thing he'd mentioned that I knew. I'd been there once as a child. It was where I'd first been introduced to William. It would be fascinating to see how much had changed.

"Then we most certainly shall. And lastly, I have us booked for an early dinner reservation at The Witchery. It's an Edinburgh tradition, and I know you'll enjoy it. Is there anything you want to change?"

I wished to do everything he mentioned, but I hated the idea of him repeating activities he'd already experienced many times for my sake.

"No, though I do have a question for ye. Have ye done all of these things before?"

He nodded and stuffed the list into his pocket before buttoning up his coat.

"Yes, but I enjoy doing them every year, so don't worry about that."

"There must be something ye wish to do in Edinburgh that ye havena done before. Whatever 'tis, let's do it after dinner."

"I know exactly what he needs to do." Emilia's voice interrupted as she made her way over to me. "Malcolm desperately needs an education in real Scotch. I've taught Kraig everything I know, but I've never had the opportunity to do the same with Malcolm. I know just the place the two of ye can go. They stay open late, and they offer tours that give ye more to taste than the wee sips most distilleries do. He'd love it."

I didn't even look up at Malcolm as I answered her.

"Aye, 'tis perfect. Every foreigner needs a proper introduction to Scottish whisky. Can ye arrange it for us?"

She gave me a quick nod and turned to address her brother-in-law.

"Malcolm, I'll text ye the address and time I've booked ye for in a while. Now, get out of here and have a grand time. I'm sure the two of ye will be out late. We will see ye tomorrow morning."

***

With his head already starting to ache and his feet far less steady than he liked, Malcolm had only two questions.

First—why couldn't they have gone on a basic whisky tasting tour—one where they only got to taste the smallest sip of each whisky? Such a tour would've sufficed just fine. Second—how the hell was Kenna still standing? She'd drunk just as much as he had and showed no signs of intoxication. She was one of the daintiest women he'd ever seen. Short of stature, slender, all of her features were petite. How then, was she drinking him under the table?

Thankfully, as their host reached for their glasses to pour yet another dram of whisky, Kenna reached out a hand to stop him. Malcolm simply couldn't drink another drop.

"Thank ye, sir, but I believe my companion here has had all he can manage." She leaned over the counter playfully and whispered below her breath as she giggled. "He's American."

Perhaps, she was more affected by the tasting than he originally thought. Still, she was holding her liquor far better than he was.

"Kenna." He spoke slowly and with intention. He'd be damned before he slurred his words in front of her. He was a grown man and one that didn't drink often. He'd not have himself looking like a lush. "We can't drive back. The car is safe where I parked it this morning. Do you want to step outside and hail us a taxi while I pay for the bottle we are bringing back to Emilia and Kraig?"

Confusion and something resembling panic crossed Kenna's rosy cheeks, but before he could inquire into her concern, their tour host stepped in.

"No need. We've cars waiting out front. 'Tis customary on this specific tour. Rarely do we have a guest that is fit to drive afterwards."

Had this been Emilia's intention? Malcolm couldn't help but think that it must've been.

Kenna held tightly onto his arm as she stood from the barstool and waited for him.

"Shall we go then? Ye doona look so good, Malcolm."

He didn't feel so good.

"Yes, I think we should."

Just as their guide had promised, a car awaited them outside the distillery. With Kenna snuggled warmly into him on the ride back to his brother's house, he found it difficult to stay awake. Just as the car pulled up to the front of the house, Kenna leaned up to kiss his cheek.

"I had the best time tonight, Mac. Truly, I dinna ever want today to end."

Paying the driver, he stepped outside and took Kenna's hand. Emilia had left the outside light on for them. Walking up to the front door, he paused and leaned in to kiss her. She melted against him instantly. It was all he could do to remain of sound mind. He wanted to be with her more than he'd wanted anything in his life —but not tonight, not when both of them were exhausted from their day in the city and more than a little tipsy.

"I'm not sure I've ever had more fun with anyone, Kenna.

Now..." Pulling away while he still had the wits to do so, he turned to insert the key into the lock. "I must bid you goodnight the moment we step inside. Otherwise, I'll ask you to come to bed with me."

He expected her to reprimand him. Instead, as they stepped inside, she took his hand and led him over to the couch where his bed was all set up.

"I doona mean to offend ye, Mac, but even if I did join ye here this evening, I believe ye would be asleep before ye could undress me."

Perhaps she was right. His lids did feel very heavy. Gently, she guided him down to the couch, pushing his shoulders back until he was lying down. She moved to pull off his shoes. He didn't want to fall asleep until she was gone. He wanted to see her every moment he could.

"Kenna, what surprised you most about today?"

Setting his shoes next to the couch, she moved to sit next to him, gently brushing the hair from his face as she leaned in to gently kiss him goodnight. After a quick peck on his lips, she stood and answered him as she made her way upstairs.

"Besides learning that ye canna hold yer whisky, ye mean? I think perhaps 'twas Edinburgh Castle. It truly hasna changed all that much in the last three hundred some odd years."

By the time her words made their way through his whisky-doused brain and he realized the oddity of them, she was gone.

He fell asleep dreaming of the castle and what Kenna could've possibly meant by such a strange statement.

CHAPTER 14

Several nights of sleep deprivation and a day filled with a flurry of activity seemed to have caught up with Malcolm when I woke the next morning. I slept pretty late myself and took my time getting ready before wandering downstairs. When I finally did make my way downstairs, Malcolm still slept soundly on the couch, despite the noise from Kraig, Emilia, and little Robbie in the kitchen.

It made me feel better to see him sleeping. The foolish mistake I'd made came to me in the middle of the night, causing me to sit up in bed in such a panic that it had taken well over an hour for me to calm myself and go back to sleep. My last words to Malcolm before going to bed—while clearly a result of too much whisky—could've been disastrous had he not been so altered by drink himself. The fact that he still slept gave me some hope that he wouldn't remember my words when he did wake.

"Good morning, Kenna. Ye look better than I expected ye to. I doona believe I'll be able to say the same for Mac when he wakes."

I gratefully took the cup of tea Emilia extended in my

direction and moved to sit by Robbie who was strapped into the most ingenious invention—a seat and a table in one that kept him upright and able to sit at the kitchen table with everyone else without being held.

"I believe ye are right. The poor man doesna drink often, 'twas plain to see." I paused as I reached out to take little Robbie's hand, smiling as his chubby fingers wrapped around mine. "Why, Robbie looks fine and happy this morning in his...his..." I stalled on purpose, hoping that Emilia would simply believe that I'd forgotten the word and would answer my question that way. She didn't disappoint me.

"His highchair."

"Aye, highchair. The word slipped my mind for a moment."

She laughed and set a plate of breakfast down in front of me.

"whisky will do that to ye. Did the two of ye have a good time yesterday?"

I waited until she and Kraig were both seated with their food before I began to eat.

"Aye, there wasna a single activity that I dinna love. He couldna have planned a better day out."

"I'm so glad the two of ye had a good time. I canna remember the last time Kraig and I had a day out just the two of us. I wouldna trade Robbie for the world, but he has changed my life in every way. Sometimes, I canna remember the woman that I was before him."

Emilia sighed in a dreamy way that caused me to really study her for the first time. While fatigue couldn't fade the young woman's beauty, the sleep deprivation that comes to any parent of a small child had left its mark. Small bags hung under her eyes. I doubted she'd taken any time for herself in months.

I had an idea, although I knew I couldn't manage it by myself.

"Emilia, do ye have a phone I could borrow and perhaps a computer I could use? I'd like to check on some things and call my grandson."

I only knew what a computer was from seeing it at Morna's and only knew how to operate a phone because of the detailed instructions Cooper had given me before I left, including the number to Morna's so I could reach him.

Emilia stood without hesitation, and I momentarily regretted interrupting her meal.

"O'course. I'm sure the lad will be glad to hear from ye. Follow me into Kraig's office. 'Tis just off the kitchen. There is a phone in there, and ye can use the computer for whatever ye like. Ye can even bring yer breakfast with ye if ye wish. Kraig eats in there all the time."

Lifting my plate with one hand and holding my tea with the other, I followed her, the surprise taking form in my mind as we went.

"*F*or the love of God, Emilia, please tell me you have some aspirin."

Squinting, Malcolm trudged into the kitchen. He couldn't remember the last time he'd slept so late or felt so rotten.

"Look there."

His gaze traveled to the place on the table where his sister-in-law pointed.

"I've already set some aspirin next to yer breakfast. Along with some coffee and a secret mixture that will taste awful but will have ye feeling just like yerself by lunch."

Malcolm sat at the table, popped the painkillers, and looked squeamishly at the glass of gray liquid sitting next to his coffee.

"What's in it?"

"Dinna ye hear what I said? 'Tis a secret. Just drink it. I promise, ye will be glad ye did."

Pinching his nose to keep from smelling the vile concoction, he chugged it in two swift gulps. As soon as it was down, he reached for his coffee and drank. He didn't care if it was hot enough to burn him, he needed the taste of the previous liquid out of his mouth immediately.

"That was the worst thing I've ever tasted. Where's Kenna? Did you make her drink that?"

Emilia laughed and leaned against the kitchen island.

"Kenna dinna need it. And she's in Kraig's office. She said she wished to call her grandson and needed to take care of a few things on the computer."

Hoping that Kenna would still be on the phone and that perhaps he would be able to say hello to Rosie, Malcolm scarfed down his food and stood to head to the office.

He knocked lightly, but when there was no answer he stepped quietly inside, standing back while Kenna spoke.

"What is the name of the place that Jane always says she misses, Cooper?"

There was a short pause, and then Kenna answered the boy, excitement in her voice.

"Aye, a spa. And how do I find and plan a spa?"

Another short pause as Malcolm watched on in amazement. Could she really not know about all of the things Cooper was explaining to her?

"What is a 'google'? Can I call this google? Oh...I must type it on the computer."

He continued to watch with amusement as Kenna typed one finger at a time on the keyboard.

"Cooper, if I arrange this, should I just give Emilia the cash to pay for it?"

Malcolm could barely hear the boy's voice, but it was just mumbling from so far away.

"Oh, I see. I need one of those credit cards. I doona have one."

He couldn't keep quiet any longer. She was clearly struggling, and he could see by the way she held one hand up to the side of her face that overwhelm was setting in. With the mention of a credit card, he saw his opening.

"I have one. What is it that you're trying to do, Kenna?"

Turning toward him, Kenna smiled. The relief on her face was evident.

"Ah, Cooper, never mind, lad. Mac is awake now. I believe I can get him to help me."

Now that he stood right next to her, he could hear the boy clearly.

"Oh, good. I was about to have to hand the phone to Morna. You were getting into stuff I don't know anything about."

Kenna laughed and held the phone away from her so he could hear better.

"Aye, well ye needn't bother Morna now. Are ye having a good time, Cooper? How is Rosie doing?"

"Oh, I'm having the best time, though I still haven't been able to get Rosie to warm to me. Not to worry though, she'll crack eventually. And Rosie's having a good time, too, I think. She and Morna have been spending so much time in the kitchen baking up all sorts of yummy goodies. I think by the time you and Malcolm get back, Jerry might be as fat as Santa Claus."

Malcolm always loved the way Kenna laughed, but when laughing in response to her grandson, there was a special joy in her voice that caused his heart to skip just a little. He knew the kind of love she felt when speaking to him. The love of a grandparent for a grandchild surpassed anything he'd felt in his life.

"I'm so glad, Cooper. Is Rosie around? I'm sure Mac would like to speak to her."

"Actually..." Cooper's voice sounded regretful. "She and Morna went into town to get some more baking stuff. There's no telling what they will make next."

85

Malcolm lowered his head and spoke into the phone to calm Cooper's worries.

"It's okay, Cooper, I'm sure Rosie is enjoying having some space away from me for a bit. I'll see her tomorrow when we return."

"Sounds good. I miss both of you guys. Good luck planning your surprise."

Malcolm waited to speak again until Kenna said her goodbyes and hung up the phone.

"So...what is it you are trying to do? Why would you need to give Emilia cash?"

Malcolm listened to Kenna intently. As she laid out her plan to give Kraig and Emilia a day and evening away, he knew that what he'd been trying to silence inside of himself for the better part of two days was true. He was in love with Kenna McMillan. He might not know her well, but he knew enough. She was kind, funny, and thoughtful. She loved her grandson deeply and said whatever was on her mind. He knew what he'd told her before, but it was no longer true. He was fairly certain that it hadn't been true then. He wouldn't be able to let her go tomorrow. He wasn't sure that he would ever be able to.

"Did ye...did ye hear me? Ye doona look as if ye heard a word I said. Will ye help me? Do ye mind if we stay here this evening and watch the babe for them?"

Shaking himself from his thoughts, he smiled and bent to kiss her.

"I heard every word. Of course, I'll help you. I can't think of anything else Emilia would want more this Christmas. Scoot over. I'll get everything set while you go and tell them to pack a bag for the night."

Kenna stood without a word and all but skipped away from him in excitement.

He called out to her just before she left the room.

"And Kenna...don't let Emilia turn this offer down. She will try to."

"Oh, doona ye worry about that, Malcolm. I always get my way. I doona know what 'tis exactly, but people have always had a difficult time telling me no."

He knew precisely what it was. The woman contained magic, surely, and he was entirely under her spell.

CHAPTER 15

W hile I hadn't noticed the black dress until after I arrived in the twenty-first century—for I surely would've had Adelle remove it immediately if I had—I was grateful it was there as I readied myself for the evening while Malcolm worked at preparing dinner for the two of us in the kitchen.

I felt naked in the dress with the bottom hem hitting just at my knees. I'd never worn anything that showed so much of my legs. And the cut at the top was even more scandalous. I was now showing even more than I'd revealed to Malcolm the day my blouse had burst open during my nap. Still, I thought I looked quite beautiful in the dress. I hoped Malcolm would think so, too.

If I didn't wake with the dewy skin Adelle was so sure I needed after wearing this tonight, there was nothing that would get Malcolm to sleep with me.

Slipping on the pair of heels, which were another twenty-first century invention I could see no sense in, I reached for the lipstick I'd yet to wear and carefully applied it before heading downstairs.

I spent the better part of two hours feeding, changing, and

bouncing the child before he finally fell asleep. I very much hoped he would at least give us a handful of hours of alone time before he woke up in need of some attention.

"Kenna..." Malcolm's tone was nearly breathless. "You are the most beautiful woman I've ever seen."

I felt almost ill at how quickly my body warmed in response to his words. He looked rather handsome himself, though he wasn't dressed up as I was.

"That canna be true, but I'll accept the compliment. Thank ye. What are ye making?"

"Braised beef in a cherry sauce with crisped onions and asparagus. It's the only dish I know how to make well."

"I'm sure 'twill be delicious."

I walked over to wrap my arms around him, but he quickly stepped out of my way.

"It's nearly ready. Let me step into the bathroom and change. You look so nice. I don't want to look like a slob next to you."

I grabbed his hand and pulled him back toward me.

"No, doona change. No one will see us. I only wore this for ye and I think ye look handsome dressed just as ye are."

His response was immediate. A low, guttural noise escaped from deep within his throat. Pulling me against him, he kissed me greedily, allowing his hands to roam my body in a way he never had before.

I gasped and moaned in response, pressing one of my breasts into his palm as his hand slipped down my chest while his other hand roamed down to cup my bottom.

"Mom?"

Thinking that I'd just found the fault in him I'd been waiting for, I stilled and pulled away. I should've realized by the inflection in his tone, but it took me far too long to catch on.

"Malcolm, while I am a mother, I am not yer mother and the thought of ye referring to me as 'Mom' makes my skin crawl all over. Perhaps we should cease this and just eat."

Malcolm's expression looked horrified.

"God, no, Kenna. I would sooner die than call you Mom. It's my actual mother. She's here."

An unsettling mixture of relief and embarrassment rushed over me as I turned to see an astonishingly beautiful elderly woman standing no more than ten steps from us. As I locked eyes with her, she lifted her hand and waved before giving me the biggest smile I'd ever seen in my life.

CHAPTER 16

"*E*xcuse me. I believe I hear Robbie upstairs. I best go and check on him."

Malcolm waited until Kenna was out of view to address his mother. The moment he turned toward her, his mother pursed her lips guiltily.

"I am so sorry, Malcolm. Kraig told me that you had a lady friend here tonight, but it truly never crossed my mind that she was anything more than a friend."

He'd known that Kenna was bound to meet his mother sometime during her stay in Edinburgh. He only wished his mother's timing was better.

"Why would you assume that?"

She lifted her brows and looked up at him knowingly.

"Well, it's been a very long time, son. Forgive me if that isn't where my mind went right away. I am sorry for intruding though. If there's anything I can do to make it up to you, just say the word."

As if on cue, Robbie let out a bloodcurdling scream that reverberated down the stairway. He didn't even have to ask the question before his mother stood and brushed off her lap.

"Absolutely. It's been months since Emilia has allowed me to take Robbie overnight. I believe she feels guilty asking me because she knows that I raised babies much later in life than most. As if that is her fault, of all things. I'll go and take the child from Kenna now. Start cleaning the kitchen. It will increase your chances greatly. Nothing turns a woman on more than the sight of a man doing dishes."

Thankful that his mother's shocking remarks had lost their effect on him ages ago, he did as instructed. He loved his mother, but he'd never been so ready for her to be out of his sight.

I'd rocked and bounced my fair share of babies, but never had I seen one so upset. Robbie screamed endlessly. With each new wail, I knew my hopes for what this night could be were now squandered.

"There is nothing wrong with his lungs, is there?"

I half-smiled, half-grimaced as Malcolm's mother, Nel, stepped into the nursery and closed the door behind her.

"Aye, I doona believe the wee lad is accustomed to being away from his mother."

"Oh no, not at all. It won't last forever, of course. I think it's something that most first-time mothers go through, but Emilia rarely wants to be separated from him for more than a few hours. The fact that she agreed to let you and Malcolm watch him overnight is proof of just how exhausted she must be."

"I've not heard her complain once since I've been here, but aye, I do believe fatigue was beginning to take its toll."

I stood from my seat and cradled the baby as I began to swing him side to side. Slowly, his wails began to subside.

"How many grandchildren do you have?"

I couldn't help but smile when thinking about each and every one of them.

"Five."

"And how many children do you have?"

"Three." The sharp, familiar pang that always coursed through me at the thought of Niall ran its way up and down my body. "But one of my sons passed away a few years ago."

Nel's expression was immediately sympathetic. "I'm so sorry."

She glanced down in the way that people often did at hearing such news and shifted from foot to foot for a moment as she looked for a way to transition to a more pleasant conversation. Eventually, she spoke again.

"I am sorry for interrupting your evening. To make up for the intrusion, I've decided to take Robbie with me back to my place across the street. I believe you two probably need some alone time."

The embarrassment I felt at knowing that Malcolm's mother knew what we were up to caused me to immediately regret every instant I'd been so straightforward about such matters with my own sons' significant others. I was always so blunt with them—it couldn't have been very comfortable for them to hear me speak of such things. I certainly wasn't comfortable now.

I fumbled over my words as I tried to respond to her.

"Oh...um...that 'tisn't necessary. Truly."

She reached forward and pulled Robbie from my arms, sending him into a fit of screams, once again.

"I believe it is. Kenna, it was wonderful to meet you. I haven't seen my son so happy in a very long time. Please don't hurt him."

My heart squeezed familiarly in response to her plea. I knew precisely what it felt like to worry over the well being of a child's heart.

"I doona wish to hurt him." I paused, unsure of why I felt compelled to explain anything to her. "But, we are from verra different worlds. I'm not sure there is anything either of us can do about that."

"There is always something to be done. You only have to decide whether or not you want to put forth the effort."

Turning before I could respond, she turned and fled the room, leaving me to think on all she'd said.

I wanted to be with Malcolm this night—I wouldn't deny myself that—but deep down I knew sleeping with him could only have two possible results. Tomorrow I would either wake happy and full of clarity, or I would wake utterly and completely miserable with confusion.

CHAPTER 17

I took my time before joining Malcolm downstairs. I needed a few moments to reset my mood—to open myself up to the possibility of intimacy once again. After taking a quick glance in the mirror, I nervously made my way to the staircase. Malcolm stood in the living room, in front of the fireplace as he stoked away at the logs he'd just added to the fire.

"I wasn't sure at first, but it turns out her surprise visit wasn't such a terrible thing after all, was it."

He must've heard my footsteps for he didn't turn and look at me as I approached. Hesitantly, I wrapped my arms around him from behind and pressed myself against him for warmth.

He sighed, hung the fire poker back on its hook, and turned into me, winding his hands through my hair as he did so.

"It must be near morning now. It felt as if she was here forever."

Laughing, I leaned back to bare my neck to him as he bent to kiss it.

"I doona believe she even stayed an hour. We still have the whole night."

Malcolm ceased his soft touches up and down my neck as he pulled away and regarded me sternly.

"Thank God for that. For, Kenna, I plan to spend the rest of the night exploring and tasting every last inch of you. That is…" He hesitated, and I didn't miss how his lower lip trembled just slightly. "If you'll allow me."

I wanted to be with him in every way that I possibly could.

Smiling, I nodded and reached for the collar of his shirt.

"I want ye to make love to me, Malcolm. Over and over again until I am too blissfully weary to do anything other than sleep."

In answer, he gently spun me away from him, and gently pulled down the zipper at the back of my dress. It hung loosely at my shoulders, and he moved his lips to my cheek kissing it softly before dragging his tongue down the arch of my neck. I shivered at the sensation as his hands slipped through the opening in the back of my dress, sliding against my bare skin.

I gasped as his hands cupped my breasts. When he moved to gently tug at my nipple with his fingers, I moaned and leaned into him.

He shifted and my dress began to slip. Instinctively, my arms jerked upward to prevent its fall.

"Wait."

Malcolm stilled immediately, quickly withdrawing his hands before stepping away from me.

"What is it? Do you want me to stop?"

With arms crossed over my front to keep the dress up, I faced him.

"No. The verra last thing I want ye to do is stop. 'Tis only that I'm frightened, Mac. I havena…'tis been a verra long time since anyone saw me naked."

Relief washed over Malcolm's face as he smiled and stepped close to me, wrapping his arms around me in an embrace that helped to melt away my fears.

"Come here, Kenna."

He turned and walked to the couch, leaving me to follow him as I continued to cling to the front of my dress.

Once I was seated next to him, he placed his hands on the sides of my face and kissed me until I was warm and tingling all over. When he pulled away, his voice was strained with need. "I don't think any man enjoys vulnerability, Kenna, but for you I will lay myself bare. I am frightened too. So frightened that if I weren't pressing my legs into the ground right this second, I'm afraid my legs might tremble. It's been a very long time for both of us. There is no need for us to rush tonight. I will take as much time as you wish me to."

Knowing that I wasn't alone in my nerves was all I needed to hear. Rising, I allowed the dress to fall down to my waist as I crawled into his lap and began to kiss him.

True to his word, and ever the gentleman, he did take his time, undressing himself before pulling the dress off me completely and laying me backwards on the makeshift bed. We explored and tasted one another slowly. When we finally did come together, it was all I could do to keep from weeping at the pleasure that rolled over and through me as we rocked together in unison.

I'd heard whisperings of what lovemaking could be between a man and a woman—the feelings one could experience when two people came together as one.

Until now, I'd never experienced it for myself.

I would never, ever be the same.

Thoroughly sated, deliriously happy, and now rather hungry, Malcolm sat across from Kenna by the fire where they both sat draped in sheets as they munched on a bag of microwave popcorn and sipped on glasses of wine. While he didn't believe that either of them had ever held much back from another, their shared intimacy had opened them both up in a way that had them sharing with each other like never before. He could scarcely believe his ears now.

"You can't be serious. Ever?"

Kenna smiled, laughed, and popped a handful of kernels in her mouth. He loved that she didn't wait to finish eating to answer him. She spoke as she munched, and it made him feel even closer to her.

"Aye, I am verra serious. I always knew it was supposed to be possible, but my late husband was never overly concerned with how pleasurable the experience might be for me. Sex was for creating our children, little more."

Malcolm shook his head in disbelief. What sort of a fool could show her such little care?

"The man sounds like a damned moron."

Kenna reached for a log behind her and tossed it into the fire as she laughed.

"I'll not speak ill of my sons' father, but I willna disagree with ye, either. Do ye know, Malcolm, thinking on the young girl I'd once been, I believe I know the sort of man I would've chosen for myself had I been given the choice. I believe it would've been someone like ye—someone who knew how to show strength and gentleness in equal measure, someone who showed kindness in all things, and who knew how to laugh. Someone who made me feel wanted."

He was certain he'd never been given such a kind compliment. He hardly saw himself in such a good light.

"I wish I had known you then, Kenna. Or, at the very least, I wish I'd met you ten years ago, when we were both far enough past the loss of our spouses to be open to new love. It would've given us so much more time than we can ever have now."

A sadness crossed Kenna's face, and the melancholy feeling quickly spread through Malcolm, as well.

"Kenna..." He paused, not wanting to ruin the evening but knowing they couldn't avoid the conversation forever. "Did you mean what you told me before? Do you really intend for this to end when I drop you off at Morna and Jerry's tomorrow?"

She scooted near him and leaned into his chest.

"I doona want it to be over, but I must see first. There is someone I must speak to, to see what might be possible."

Who besides the two of them would need to have any say in how things progressed? Malcolm couldn't imagine, but he knew better than to question her too much.

"I want you to know, Kenna, I will want you for as long as you want me. Whatever happens from here on out is entirely up to you."

And he meant it. If she would have him, he was hers. He would do anything he needed to do to make it work.

He only hoped she would give him the chance.

CHAPTER 18

The drive from Edinburgh to Morna and Jerry's the next morning was an awkward one. We were both exhausted, and the great joy of the night before seemed to put a damper on our feelings of today. Neither of us knew for sure where our relationship would go from here and the uncertainty had us both out of sorts.

I'd already decided that I wanted Malcolm in my life for much longer than the end of today, but until I spoke with Morna, I couldn't know for sure if my hopes were foolish. How many families could Morna safely expose her magic to? Our relationship would put her most at risk. I would say nothing to Malcolm until I spoke to her.

I rode for the first hour thinking about all of the possibilities—all of the ways Morna might respond to my request. Thankfully, Malcolm eventually spoke, breaking the silence and providing me with a distraction from my nervous thoughts.

"Kenna, do you remember how when we got to Edinburgh, you mentioned that you could arrange a tour of McMillan Castle for Rosie and me?"

I'd forgotten, but I'd most assuredly meant every word. Kamden and Harper would both be thrilled to show them around.

"Aye, were ye thinking about taking Rosie there on yer way back? 'Tis out of the way, but 'tis worth the trip."

He smiled at me and reached over to squeeze my hand. The simple contact seemed to ease the tension inside the car—as if his touch broke through an invisible barrier between us.

"Yes, that's what I was thinking. I know she won't be happy to leave. I hoped that if I could tempt her with the promise of something I know she's wanted to see for a while, she might make it a little easier on me."

"Aye, I think it could be just the thing to make leaving easier for her. I'll call them as soon as we get to Morna's."

"Thank you." He lifted my left hand and kissed it. I leaned toward him as much as the barrier in between our seats would allow.

"'Tis no trouble at all."

"Kenna..." He paused the way he often did before asking me a question. It seemed to be a habit of his. I found it rather endearing.

"Aye?"

"There's a question that has been on my mind since the first night I met you, but there hasn't really been an appropriate time to ask it. I'm afraid it will make you sad, but I'd very much like to know."

He had to know that after such a statement, any female would be too curious to discourage whatever his question might be. Whatever could he ask me that would make me sad?

"Being sad shall hardly kill me. Ask whatever 'tis."

"That first night we met, when I thanked you for not showing me pity, you said you'd experienced your own share of grief. I know you lost your husband, but after all you've said of him, I think you must've meant something more."

Knowing that I intended to share more of my life with him meant that I wanted him to truly know me—to know and understand my wounds as well as my joys.

"Aye, I did. The grief I referred to...a few years ago I lost a son."

I'd never spoken of Niall to anyone outside of my family, and I hardly knew how to do so now.

"My son wasna a good man. He had an evil in him that I was blind to for far too long. While I refuse to take responsibility for his actions, I do sometimes wonder." My voice caught as the inevitable lump rose in the back of my throat. Turning away, I allowed the tears to fall as I continued. "I...I sometimes wonder if I had I seen who he really was sooner, perhaps I could have done something to prevent everything that happened."

Without a word, the car slowed as Malcolm pulled to a stop on the side of the road. He waited until I faced him to speak.

"I will show you the same courtesy that you showed me. I will give you no pity, but I don't believe this is the sort of discussion one should have while driving. I want you to know that I hear you and that I recognize the strength it must've taken for you to get through something so horrible. I am sorry, Kenna. You only have to tell me what you wish to."

It was right of him to recognize that I would be as reluctant to someone's pity as he was, and I appreciated the space he created for me to tell him the story. I did so for the better part of an hour. Sobbing, I told him things that I didn't even know I needed to say out loud—things I could never say to my family, for they were too intimately connected to all that had happened. Having someone outside of the situation made it so much easier.

"I think what pains me the most is the undeniable truth that I still love him. I shouldna love such a monster. But even years since his passing, even knowing that he murdered my first daughter-in-law, knowing that he murdered my sister and tried to kill his brother and me, I still love him fiercely. 'Tis why it took me so long to see the truth—we mothers always believe the best of our children. Perhaps, 'tis what it means to be a mother—no matter the joy it can bring, it can also be the most painful thing in the world."

Malcolm had tears in his eyes, too, but not tears of pity—his gaze made that clear. They were the tears of empathy. While one separates, the other binds. I'd not thought it possible for me to feel closer to him than I had last night, but in some way this story was even more personal than sharing my body with him. I'd never felt so close to anyone.

"Of course you still love him. Love, once truly given, doesn't ever go away. And there is no truer love than that of a parent for their child."

He brushed the hair from my face and stroked my cheek as I drew in shaky breaths.

I knew I needed no one's permission to love Niall, but just hearing Malcolm acknowledge that it was okay made me feel so much less alone. I felt free for the first time in years, as if some poison within me had finally been flushed away.

"I've never cried in front of anyone the way I just cried in front of ye, but now I'm quite ready to stop. Do ye know any good jokes, Malcolm?"

He chuckled just a little and raised his brows mischievously.

"Not a one, but I think I know of something that might put a smile back on that beautiful face of yours."

I was open to anything.

"What?"

He grinned and reached to open the door on his side of the car.

"Get out for a minute. I'll show you."

No sooner did I step out of the vehicle than I was smacked directly in the middle of my chest with a giant snowball.

Chaos ensued as we played and wrestled in a giant field of snow just off the road in the middle of nowhere.

We arrived at Morna and Jerry's two hours later than expected, soaked through, looking utterly a mess, and blissfully happy by each other's side.

CHAPTER 19

*O*ur late arrival at the inn changed everyone's plans—not that anyone minded. Rather than head to McMillan Castle for their tour today, Malcolm and Rosie would leave tomorrow. The extra time together gave me hope that I would be able to speak with Morna before they left, and one way or another I would be able to tell Malcolm how things could move forward.

While the days spent together had made Cooper tolerable to Rosie, it was evident that it would still take much convincing for her to consider him a friend. Ever the determined young lad, Cooper wasn't worried in the least.

"Nana, I think I'm in love."

"Really?" Smiling at him as he entered my room, I patted the bed so he would come and sit down. I'd just finished drying my hair from the snow fight and was carefully applying just a little bit of make-up so I would look presentable for dinner. "What makes you think so?"

"Do you remember when Dad was falling in love with Kathleen?"

I nodded, laid the lipstick down, and faced my grandson.

"Aye."

"He was so grumpy and strange, but he still wanted to be around her. That's how I feel now, Nana. I shouldn't want to be around someone that dislikes me so much, but..." he held up both palms and shrugged as he shook his head, "for some reason, I kinda like it that she's so mean to me."

Laughing, I moved to pull him into a hug.

"'Tis something I will never understand, but it seems to be common amongst men, Cooper. Perhaps, ye are right. Ye may have gotten yer first taste of love."

He pulled away and grinned up at me with excited eyes.

"Should I tell her?"

Panic ran through me as I dropped to my knees to discourage him.

"Ach, no lad, I wouldna do that if I were ye. I doona think Rosie would take to it well, and while those first feelings of love can be verra powerful and they come on verra fast, they also often pass just as quickly."

Thankfully, Cooper didn't seem bothered by my dissuasion. He nodded as if he understood and moved toward the doorway.

"Okay, good thinkin', Nana. I'll wait."

"Good, I truly think that best, Cooper. Are ye headed downstairs?"

He nodded and reached for the doorknob.

"If Morna isna busy, will you ask her to come up here? I'd really like to speak to her."

"Sure thing, Nana. She's not busy. She's just watching Rosie cook. She's gonna make the whole thing by herself tonight."

There was such admiration in Cooper's voice when he spoke of Rosie. There was no question—my grandson had found his very first crush.

*T*he smells coming from the kitchen were wonderful. Situating his bag next to his pallet on the living room floor, a freshly showered and dry Malcolm called out to Morna to see if he could offer some help.

"Morna, that smells fantastic. Is there anything I can do to help you?"

Rosie's voice answered him.

"It's me, Pops. Morna's not in here."

He stepped into the kitchen to see his granddaughter smiling the first true smile he'd seen on her since arriving in Scotland. Standing proud in front of the stove, she wore an apron that hung just a little too long. It didn't matter that she had to stand on her tiptoes to look down at the food, she appeared to know exactly what she was doing.

"Are you making all of this yourself?"

She reached for a spoon, dipped it into the pot she worked over, then carefully balanced it over her hand as she walked over to him.

"Yes. Morna watched me for a little while just to make sure I didn't have any questions, but when she saw I had it mastered, she went to go see Kenna. She's letting me do everything on my own tonight. Here, taste it."

Taking a brief second to blow on the stew, he placed the spoonful in his mouth.

"It's delicious."

Rosie regarded him skeptically.

"Really? You don't have to lie to me."

"Really, Rosie. It's wonderful. I can't believe you learned so much in just a few days."

Malcolm would be forever grateful to Morna for the way she'd turned this holiday around for his granddaughter. It seemed the old woman had known just what Rosie needed.

"Morna is a great teacher, Pops. She even taught me how to

read UK recipes. They use measurements that are pretty different than how we do things back home, but it didn't take me long to get the hang of it. It actually makes more sense than what we use. Pops..." Rosie laid down the spoon and surprised him by wrapping her arms around his waist. "Thank you for letting me stay. I know I wasn't very nice to you. I'm sorry. I was just...I was just sad."

He bent to kiss the top of her head. If he loved the child any more than he already did, he worried his heart would burst from it.

"I know, kiddo. It's okay to be sad. Just a few more days and then your Mom should be here."

"I hope so, Pops. I really, really do. But even if she doesn't come, this has already been one of my favorite Christmases ever."

"Well, it sounds like you need to thank Morna for that, Rosie."

"No, Pops. It's not Morna that made this great. It was you. If you hadn't tried to cheer me up by booking that tour to Conall Castle, we would've never stayed here."

The decision had been so last minute. All he'd wanted was to get Rosie out of the house in the hopes of making her smile. How could he have possibly known that such an outing would change so much for both of them?

Even if things didn't turn out how he hoped, he would treasure his time spent with Kenna for the rest of his life.

"You know what, Rosie? This has already been one of my favorite Christmases, too."

CHAPTER 20

"*D*id ye really believe for a moment that I would say ye couldna tell him, Kenna?"

I didn't know Morna as well as many of the members of my family. While I knew she often allowed matters of the heart to direct her decisions, in my mind, it was still entirely possible that she could reject my suggestion.

"I dinna know."

Morna patted my knee in a motherly fashion.

"Lass, 'twas I who encouraged ye to see if the two of ye had something together. It pleases me more than ye know that ye do. I thought on this quite a lot while ye were in Edinburgh. As ye know, there have been many I've had to share my magic with over the years, and if one thing is for certain, 'tis rarely knowledge they accept easily. I think I know of a way that might make him more accepting."

I'd seen first hand what a difficult time Grace's sister, Jane, in particular, had with learning of time travel and the magic that surrounded pretty much all who knew Morna. If the old witch had any idea as to how to make it easier for Malcolm to accept, I would allow her to direct our next steps.

"Morna, ye have done this many more times than I. Whatever ye wish me to do, I shall do it."

"Good. Pack yer bags and tell Cooper to do the same. When Malcolm and Rosie leave in the morning, we are going to McMillan Castle with them."

"Are ye so ready to be rid of us, Morna? Ye do know that Cooper and I were meant to stay with ye for another week, aye?"

"Aye, I know 'twas the original plan, but it no longer fits with what needs to be done. Ye need to be at McMillan Castle with Malcolm. If ye and Cooper will be headed there anyway, ye may as well go home afterward."

While Cooper was normally very sympathetic to the needs of others, he wouldn't be so forgiving of anyone who shortened his time with Morna.

"I canna do that to Cooper, Morna. He's looked forward to his time here for so long."

Morna stood, quickly dismissing my concern.

"Doona worry about that, lass. Much as I loathe to admit it, I lost a bet with the lad, and my loss has caused me to do something that I've sworn more than once I wouldna do again."

I knew from experience that it was never a good idea to make bets with Cooper. He never forgave a debt, and I knew of only one thing that Morna had vocally promised to never do again.

"Ye canna mean...?"

"Aye. I hope the wee lad knows how much I love him, for he is the only one that could get me to agree to go back once again. It seems Jerry and I will be spending Christmas in the year 1651."

"Oh, Morna!" I stood and threw my arms around her as she laughed. "I've not heard such good news in a verra long time. Everyone at the castle will be so excited. We must send word to everyone—all of the relatives—and have them come stay, too. It will be a grand reunion. We are long overdue for one anyway."

Morna sniffled, and I pulled back with shock to see that she was crying.

"Well, if I shall be there anyway, then I would verra much love to see everyone."

Gripping her shoulders, I gave them a reassuring squeeze.

"Then we shall make certain that ye do. Now, tell me. Just how should I explain everything to Malcolm once we get to McMillan Castle?"

---

*T*he nerves I felt standing nearly naked before Malcolm were nothing compared to the nerves I felt walking into the grand room of McMillan Castle. Morna was right—it was the perfect place to tell him the truth. My likeness hung in the room, right in line with the dozens of portraits of my ancestors and the descendants that would come after me. It would be a sure way to get him curious for the portrait looked exactly like me. Only in the McMillan Castle of today, the woman in the portrait should've been dead for hundreds of years.

While it would help raise the question in his mind, he would still believe me mad. Any sane person would. Thankfully, McMillan Castle provided quick access back to my own time where I could show him in person. Morna, Kamden, and Harper were in on the plan, too. They would keep Cooper and Rosie occupied and away from this part of the castle for the next few hours—plenty of time for me to tell him what I must and also to take a quick trip back into the past to prove that all I said was true.

After that, it would be up to him. If it turned out to be too much, he and Rosie could leave, and I would officially let go of the dream of being with Malcolm.

"Where did everyone else run off to?"

"I believe they are ice skating on the pond. Then they plan to go on a carriage ride through the grounds."

His expression was quizzical.

"Are we not joining them?"

"No, Malcolm. I need to speak with ye."

"Do you intend to put me out of my misery? Please say that you are. I don't think I can stand another moment of wondering. Rosie and I leave this afternoon. I made myself very clear to you in Edinburgh. I want you. I want to be with you, and if all continues to go as well as it has the past few days, I want to enjoy the next forty years of my life with you at my side. But I need to know, Kenna...do you want me, too? Did you find whatever answers you needed—speak to whomever you needed to speak to?"

"Aye, Malcolm." I hurried to his side, reaching up to kiss him as his nearness helped my fears fade. "I want ye. I want ye more than anything I've wanted in my entire life. And aye, I spoke to whom I needed to. But there is something I must tell ye. It may change the way ye feel about our future together."

Reassuringly, he took my hands and kissed them.

"I don't think there is anything you could tell me that would do that."

Pulling one of my hands from his grip, I pointed to my portrait behind him.

"I want ye to look at that painting, Malcolm."

He turned and stared at my likeness for a long moment before speaking.

"Wow. I knew you were a McMillan, but you're a McMillan by marriage, correct? How could a McMillan ancestor resemble you so much?"

"'Tis not an ancestor. The woman in that painting is me."

Malcolm's brows pulled together in confusion, and his mouth opened and closed several times without a word.

Just as he started to speak, his phone rang.

Instinctively, I knew the call was not good news.

cMillan Castle – December of 1651
Three Days Later

I didn't cry upon returning home to my own century. It wasn't as if Malcolm had broken my heart or disbelieved my story. In truth, I'd not given him the chance to do either of those things. Malcolm's phone call from his daughter had made the absurdity of my dream for us clear.

The lives of his daughter and granddaughter were in America. Even if he loved me—which I knew he did—he would no sooner ask them to uproot their lives than I would ask my family to uproot theirs. Even if I told him about the magic, it would bring our worlds no closer together.

"Your skin looks better, but other than that, you look worse than I've ever seen you. It's been three days, Kenna. I know that you and I aren't very close, but you have to tell someone what happened while you were away. I'm nosy enough to hound you about it even though I can see you're hurting, so it might as well be me. Now spill."

BETHANY CLAIRE

It didn't surprise me in the least that Adelle would enter my room without knocking. She wouldn't leave me alone until I told her something. I would tell her only what was absolutely true. Not a word more.

"I fell in love. As foolish as it sounds, I fell in love with a great man in a matter of only a few days, but it couldna ever work. I'll not upend his world by telling him the where and how I live when our love is doomed from the start. He's gone. Back to America with his granddaughter, which is exactly where he should be. I'll not speak of this again. 'Tis too painful and I'll not be sad at Christmas for 'twould only spoil the season for everyone else. Please leave me, Adelle, and doona ask me anything else."

She must've recognized just how much my heart was aching, for in a move quite out of character for her, she turned and left me without another word.

I did cry then. It was well into the night before I fell asleep, my pillow soaked with tears.

Chicago

Malcolm was angry—angrier than he'd ever been. It made no sense. None of it. Just minutes after telling him that she wanted him more than anything she'd wanted in her life, Kenna ended things with a coldness that nearly knocked him over.

All he'd done was announce that he and Rosie would have to fly back to America before Christmas. It had been Madeline on the phone with the news he'd hoped wouldn't come, but expected anyway. She'd decided not to come to Edinburgh for Christmas,

118

after all. Despite the fact that his daughter had insisted that he and Rosie stay to enjoy Christmas in Scotland, he knew in that instant what they must do. For his daughter to believe it was acceptable for her to choose not to spend Christmas with Rosie, well, that was a line he simply wouldn't allow her to cross. His daughter needed a reality check. If that meant he would have to cut their trip short to give it to her, he would gladly do so.

He never expected such an announcement to incite such a shocking reaction from Kenna. She had children—children she loved more than life itself. He'd been so certain she would understand.

Instead, even as he tried to explain to her, to tell her that while he must go back to Chicago now, he would come back to Edinburgh for the new year so they could work things out and decide best how to make their relationship work, she'd had none of it. She ended things quickly, bidding him farewell as if he were little more than a stranger.

He still couldn't wrap his mind around the fact that it was truly over. What had happened to change her mind? And what had she been about to tell him? Her nonsense about the portrait was still a mystery. It was almost as perplexing as what she'd said to him about Edinburgh Castle on the night of the whisky tasting.

There'd been so much anticipation, so much excitement, and then in seconds, it was all gone. His heart hurt in a way he didn't know was possible.

"Dad?" His daughter's voice stirred him from his thoughts as she spoke to him from the chair next to his in the living room of their home. "Where are you? It's definitely not here."

He answered her unthinkingly. "You of all people have no right to speak to me of being away."

His daughter jerked back as if he'd slapped her. "What is that supposed to mean?

While Malcolm regretted the abrupt nature of his words, such a conversation with his daughter was long overdue. While it was always best to speak when not angry, he doubted he would feel a sense of calm ever again. And what he needed to say to Madeline was too important. If she didn't wake up from her selfishness soon, her relationship with Rosie would be irreparable.

"Madeline, you know exactly what I mean. I know that losing Tim was difficult for you and I have tried to give you the space you needed to grieve, but this has gone far beyond that. You're punishing your daughter for something that isn't her fault—you're avoiding her because she looks like him. She sees you pulling away. And as much as it breaks her heart to do so, she's pulling away from you, too. She knows that she must in order to protect herself."

Madeline's face was red and angry and tears pooled in her eyes as she answered him, her voice shaky.

"You don't know what you're talking about. I'm not punishing her. It's just...it's too hard, Dad."

His own voice rose with his anger.

"Tough. Life's hard. If you think you're the only one that has ever gone through something, then you need to pull your head out of your ass. You lost your mother when you were Rosie's age. What would it have done to you if I'd treated you the way you treat Rosie? You'd think you'd see that. It's exactly the same thing. You look just like your mother. It was hard for me, too, but I wasn't as selfish. I'm not sure I've ever known anyone as selfish as you, and I won't put up with it anymore."

"Put up with it?"

Madeline was screaming at him now, and Malcolm knew Rosie would hear them. Maybe that was okay. He wanted his granddaughter to know that he was willing to fight for her.

"Yes, Madeline. I won't put up with it."

"Put up with it?" His daughter repeated herself, the octave of her voice high and filled with venom. She was shaking all over. "This is my house, Dad. Did I ask you to move in here? No, I did not. You did it after Tim died because you insisted that I needed you. Perhaps for a time, you were right, but I don't need you anymore. Pack your things and get out. You are no longer welcome in my home."

For the second time in the span of a week, Malcolm's world collapsed.

CHAPTER 22

Christmas Day

 knock on his hotel room door woke him just past nine in the morning, Christmas Day. He hoped to spend the day sleeping. Perhaps then, he would pass the holiday without reflecting on the fact that it was his first Christmas spent alone.

Losing Kenna was difficult enough, but being away from his granddaughter on her favorite day of the year was unbearable.

"Room service. I've got your breakfast here."

The voice was strange, oddly high for anyone old enough to be working in a hotel.

Flipping the lamp on next to the bed, he called out in answer. "I didn't order any room service. You must have the wrong room."

There was a slight pause, and then, "It...It's free on Christmas Day."

Hope coursed through Malcolm's body. It almost sounded like Rosie, but of course, that couldn't be so.

"I'm not hungry."

"Oh, come on, Pops. You're really making it hard for me to surprise you. I've been up since five waiting to come and get you, but Mom made me wait until the sun was up."

Tears filled Malcolm's eyes as he stood from the bed, threw on his sweats and a shirt and ran to the door to pull his granddaughter into a hug.

"What are you doing here?"

She squirmed until he released her.

"I already told you, Pops. Mom and I have a big surprise for you. She's in the car downstairs. You gotta hurry."

Reaching for his coat, he left his other belongings in the room. Everything that he needed was right in front of him.

---

*I*nside Madeline and Rosie's home—he was no longer sure he could call it his own—Malcolm walked into a living room filled with wrapping paper. Open packages lay sprawled out all over the floor. Only one unwrapped present remained under the tree.

"What can the surprise be? You two already did the fun part without me."

"Oh, no we didn't. This wasn't nearly as exciting as your present. Mom just let me open these so I would stop bugging her about going to get you so early."

He didn't think he'd ever seen Rosie so excited about anything.

"Ah. Well, I can't imagine what it could be. Do you want me to sit?"

"You better, Pops. Otherwise, I think you might fall over."

Madeline walked up behind him and wrapped one arm around his waist, pulling him into a hug.

"Rosie, you're going to give it away if you're not careful. Why don't you grab it and bring it over here?"

As Rosie walked to the tree, Madeline turned to look up at him. "I'm so sorry. You were right about everything. That's the only reason I got so mad. I knew you were right even as I was screaming at you. I just couldn't stand what I'd done. I love you, Dad. "

"Oh, Madeline." He kissed the top of her head as if she were a small child. To him, she always would be. "I love you more than you will ever know. I'm sorry for how harsh I was. I should've gone about it another way."

"No, Dad. I don't think I would've been able to really hear it if you had. It was the first time in my life I think I saw you really, truly angry, and I believe it may have saved my life. It woke me from a fog I was in for far too long."

Rosie was back by their side, pulling at his arm to try to get him to the couch. "Come on, come on. You gotta open it now."

As soon as he sat down, Rosie placed the package in his lap. He carefully began to unwrap the paper. Rosie was bouncing up and down in her seat as he opened the box. As he looked down at the contents, all he could feel was confusion.

Packing tape, labels, and a business card for a Chicago realtor lay inside.

"Is this a polite way of telling me that you've found me a house of my own?"

Rosie leaned across him to shoot her mother a disapproving look.

"I told Mom that it wasn't nice to trick you that way. Lift that stuff up, there's something else underneath."

At the bottom of the box were two envelopes.

"Open the one on the left first, Dad."

Following his daughter's directive, he picked up the envelope on the left and carefully broke its seal. Pulling its contents free, he unfolded the papers, and read aloud, "Dear Mr. Kilmer, I would like to inform you that I am resigning my position at Mercy General Hospital effective January 7th."

He stopped and looked over at his daughter in bewilderment.

"Madeline, is this real or another part of the joke?"

Rosie answered. "It's real, Pops. I went with her when she delivered it. Now, open the other one. It's the best one."

His curiosity caused him to be less careful with the opening of the second letter. Turning the contents over so they would spill onto his lap, he stared at the tickets as he struggled to comprehend what all of this could mean.

"It's three one-way tickets to Scotland, Pops!"

"I see that, Rosie. You were right. I'm glad you told me to sit down. Now will the two of you please tell me what's going on before I lose my mind?"

Rosie pointed at her mother. "Take it away, Mom. This part's all you."

Twisting, Malcolm directed all of his attention to Madeline, his confusion giving way to curiosity and a glimmer of hope that frightened him more than he wished to admit.

"Come on, Madeline. What is this?"

"I didn't sleep for the first twenty-four hours after you left. I want you to know that I've thought through all of this. It isn't some knee-jerk decision. Rosie and I have discussed this extensively and she is one hundred percent on board."

"I sure am!"

Malcolm turned to wink at Rosie before waving his hand toward Madeline so she would continue.

"Chicago has too many memories—too much pain—for all of us. We all need a fresh start. All of our family is in Scotland now anyway. It's the only place that makes sense for us to move to. Plus, I need a slower pace of life, and the job that I've been offered sounds like just the thing that will give me that."

Malcolm could scarcely believe how quickly his worst nightmare was turning into his greatest joy.

"You already have a job?"

"Yes. As you know, Emilia's mother is the director of a home health agency that oversees a large portion of Scotland. They have need of a new nurse on the Isle of Skye, and she's offered me the job. Grandma Nel has agreed to let us all live with her in Edinburgh until Rosie and I can find the perfect place."

"Just you and Rosie?"

"Yes, Dad, just me and Rosie. Skye isn't that close to Edinburgh, but it's not all that far from McMillan Castle. Rosie told me about Kenna. That's where you need to be. It's time that I learn to stand on my own two feet. You'll still be able to see us all the time."

Sadness filled him at the mention of Kenna's name.

"Kenna doesn't want me. She made that very clear."

Rosie rose from the couch and moved to stand in front of him, blocking the space between him and Madeline.

"Don't be stupid, Pops. Of course she wants you. She just got scared is all. You gave up on that *way* too easy."

Madeline's head appeared beside Rosie's as she leaned over to speak to him.

"I don't know this Kenna, but I bet Rosie is right, so here's the plan, Dad. We will enjoy Christmas Day here together. I have a breakfast casserole and some coffee cake in the oven now. Then, you'll start packing, because your flight leaves tomorrow. Rosie and I will meet you over there after the New Year. Go and get her, Dad. It's way past time for you to be happy again."

CHAPTER 23

$\mathcal{M}$ cMillan Castle – 1651

hristmas Day was over, but the celebrations at McMillan Castle would last until after New Year's Day. With Morna and Jerry visiting us in the seventeenth century, it had taken no convincing to get all of our distant family and friends from all over Scotland to join us at the castle. The Conalls—those who had remained at their home when Bri and Adelle came — made the trip over, and all of those at Cagair Castle made the journey, as well. McMillan Castle was bursting at the seams with guests, but not one person complained. We were all thrilled to spend the holidays with those we loved most in the world.

The one downside to the large number of guests, however, was that it was nearly impossible to find a single blessed moment for one's self. I was a woman who required solitude more than just about anything. It was why my early morning hours were so precious. Even those were no longer possible—guests were staying in the room in which I always lit my morning fires.

The day after Christmas, in the late afternoon while all of the children were occupied or sleeping and their parents were outside enjoying a sleigh ride around the castle grounds, I saw my opportunity to escape to my bedchamber for just a little while.

I'd looked forward to the quiet all day, but rather than finding my room empty, I stepped inside to see what could only possibly be a ghost or a delusion.

Malcolm, dressed in clothing not suited to this time, stood a few arm lengths away.

"Wha...How?"

I stuttered as he faced me.

"Morna led me to your room. Kenna, this has been one of the longest days of my life. My head aches, and it isn't just from the time travel. Please get over here and kiss me so I will know I wasn't a fool to come all this way for you."

I nearly fell over from the shock of seeing him here. Even as I crossed the short distance between us and allowed him to take me in his arms, I couldn't make sense of it. I allowed the kiss to go on until he pulled away.

"Is this why you panicked, Kenna? You didn't want to tell me about all of this?"

I answered with my arms still wrapped around him and my face pressed against his chest. I didn't want to be away from him ever again.

"I did want to tell ye. I tried to the day ye left. 'Tis only that when yer daughter called, I knew if I told ye, 'twould be the most selfish thing I could ever do. I couldna bring myself to do it. Yer family is in America, Malcolm, and I wouldna ever ask ye to leave them. And no matter how much I love ye, ye must know that I canna ever leave my family, either. 'Tis more than just distance that separates us—time does as well."

Malcolm's hands found their way to my shoulders as he pulled me away from him so he could look straight at me.

"Do you love me, Kenna?"

The question surprised me. I thought we'd both made that abundantly clear in Edinburgh.

"Ye know that I do."

"I suspected, I hoped, but I don't believe you've ever said the words before now."

Moving my hands to his face, I stood on my tiptoes and kissed him once more.

"Well, let there be no question about it. I love ye, Malcolm, and I always shall."

Stepping away from him, reality began to set in once more.

"And while I canna tell ye just how glad I am that ye are here and that ye know of Morna's magic, it solves nothing between us. What is it that ye are doing back in Scotland, and how did ye come to know all that ye do? Ye must feel verra out of sorts."

Malcolm laughed and moved to sit on the end of the bed. He looked beyond weary. I knew how exhausting the time travel could be and I'd not experienced it the first time just seconds after learning that something I always thought impossible was very much real. Once he did fall asleep tonight, I expected he would sleep for a whole day, at least.

"I'm not sure that describes the half of it. The flight from Chicago was bad enough. My long legs are not made for eight hours on today's airplanes, and the moment I landed, I rented a car and made the long drive to McMillan Castle. I was so ready to see you, Kenna. But then I arrived only to be told that you weren't there."

"Was it Kamden and Harper that told ye the truth?"

"Yes, and I believe I owe them both an apology. I lost my patience with them. I thought they were simply making an excuse for you. I didn't believe a word until they all but forced me into the tower. Once you actually make the travel, it's rather hard to continue denying it. Kenna, how is this possible?"

I shrugged. There were so many things in life that seemed rather impossible to me.

"I doona know, but 'tis the reality of our lives around here, and if ye wish to be with me, 'twill be one of yers, as well. Do ye wish that ye dinna know?"

He still looked rather dazed. It would take days for him to fully adapt to his new perception of reality, but I was still relieved when he shook his head.

"Not at all. It explains a lot actually—your reaction to my credit card, your fascination with the lights at the symphony. Many things are beginning to click into place. I can't believe I'm in love with someone who was born over three hundred years before I was."

I didn't like the way that sounded at all.

"For the love o'God, Malcolm, doona ever say that again. Ye are older than me, in truth. Doona ye ever forget that."

He laughed then gripped his head.

"Doona worry. We do have some modern medicines here that should help that." I hesitated, but I knew that no matter how much I didn't want to hear his answer, it was a question that had to be asked. "Malcolm, what about yer family?"

"That's the thing, Kenna. It's not the issue you think it is. We're moving to Scotland—all of us. I'm already here, and Madeline and Rosie are coming just after the New Year. They will be living on Skye, which isn't all that far from here, so even with this strange business of time travel, we should be able to see them often. There's only one problem."

"Oh?" If we could be together and still be with our families, there was no other problem that was insurmountable. "What might that be?"

He stood and began to pace nervously in front of me.

"Kenna, I had a very different idea of what I was going to ask you this morning, but now after knowing what I do, I'm not sure it would be appropriate. Will you stand for a minute?"

Completely confused, I did as he asked. The moment he dropped to one knee, I jumped away from him in horror.

"Malcolm, what are ye doing? Stand up this instant."

Brows furrowed, he stood and gripped onto my bedpost for support.

"You...you don't want to marry me?"

I was suddenly getting a headache, as well. I pinched the bridge of my nose as I answered him.

"No. I love ye, Malcolm, but no. Not yet anyway. Why would ye ask that now?"

An expression I'd never seen on him before—one of pure embarrassment—crossed his face. He quickly looked down at the floor to avoid my gaze.

"I...you're right. I wasn't thinking. What I was going to ask you, what I planned to tell you before I learned that you were from the seventeenth century, was that I am currently rather homeless. I was going to ask if I could live with you for a little while. But then..." He started pacing again. "Then, when I learned that you were from the seventeenth century, I got to thinking, and it would hardly be appropriate here, would it?"

Laughing, I walked over and grabbed his hands so he would cease his wandering.

"Malcolm, there is nothing about my family that is customary or appropriate for the times. Even if it were, I've never given much concern to anyone else's opinion of how I live my life. Ye are welcome to live here as long as ye promise not to ask me to marry ye for at least another six months. And even then, I canna promise ye that I will say aye. I might find that living in sin is preferable."

His lips found mine quickly, and his aching head didn't prevent him from loving me in a way that made our night in Edinburgh seem only mediocre. If it was true that some things only got better with age, I couldn't imagine the sort of pleasure we would be able to find with one another in a decade.

It was the happiest holiday season of my whole life.

CHAPTER 24

ne Year Later
Edinburgh – Present Day

ix months to the day that Malcolm arrived in the seventeenth century, he risked rejection once again by dropping to one knee. Much to his excitement and everlasting relief, I gave him the answer he hoped for. I very much wanted to be his wife.

We wed in the prettiest little chapel either of us had ever seen, right in the center of Edinburgh. I wore a simple gold gown and Malcolm wore slacks and the sweater I first saw him in. It was intimate, with only those who knew us during our time in Edinburgh in attendance. Cooper stood at my side, while Madeline and Rosie stood at his. Morna, Jerry, Kraig, Emilia, Nel, and the toddler-terror, Robbie, watched on.

It was perfect.

At a certain age, I'd stopped hoping for much more than I had.

But there is so much more magic in the world than we can see.

Sometimes, life can surprise you in the very best possible way.

---

*E*ver since *Love Beyond Belief,* readers have asked for Raudrich Allen's story. His story is next in:

Love Beyond Words
Book 9 of Morna's Legacy Series

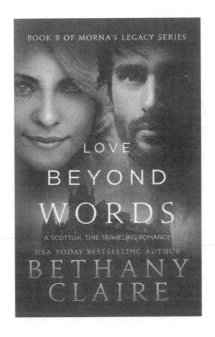

MISSED A BOOK IN THE SERIES?

SWEET/CLEAN VERSIONS OF MORNA'S LEGACY SERIES

If you enjoy sweet/clean romances where the love scenes are left behind closed doors or if you know someone else who does, check out the new sweet/clean versions of Morna's Legacy books in the Magical Matchmaker's Legacy.

Morna's Spell
Sweet/Clean Version of ***Love Beyond Time***

Morna's Secret
Sweet/Clean Version of ***Love Beyond Reason***

The Conall's Magical Yuletide

Sweet/Clean Version of *A Conall Christmas*

Morna's Magic
Sweet/Clean Version of *Love Beyond Hope*

Morna's Accomplice
Sweet/Clean Version of *Love Beyond Measure*

Jeffrey's Only Wish
Sweet/Clean Version of *In Due Time*

Morna's Rogue
Sweet/Clean Version of *Love Beyond Compare*

LETTER TO READERS

Dear Reader,

I hope you enjoyed *Morna's Magic & Mistletoe*. I love Christmas, and writing Christmas love stories is one of my favorite ways to start the holiday season. Don't stop here. Read Raudrich's story in *Love Beyond Words*.

As an author, I love feedback from readers. You are the reason that I write, and I love hearing from you. If you would like to connect, there are several ways you can do so. You can reach out to me on Facebook or on Twitter or visit my Pinterest boards. If you want to read excerpts from my books, listen to audiobook samples, learn more about me, and find some cool downloadable files related to the books, visit my website.

The best way to stay in touch is to subscribe to my newsletter. Go to my website and click the Mailing List link in the header. If you don't hear from me regularly, please check your spam folder or junk mail to make sure my messages aren't ending up there. Please set up your email to allow my messages through to you so you never miss a new book, a chance to win great prizes or a possible appearance in your area.

Finally, if you enjoyed this book, I would appreciate it so much if you would recommend it to your friends and family. And if you would please take time to review it on Goodreads and/or your favorite retailer site, it would be a great help. Reviews can be tough to come by these days, and you, the reader, have the power to make or break a book.

Thank you so much for reading my stories. I hope you choose to journey with me through the other books in the series.

All my best,

Bethany

ABOUT THE AUTHOR

BETHANY CLAIRE is a USA Today bestselling author of swoon-worthy, Scottish romance and time travel novels. Bethany loves to immerse her readers in worlds filled with lush landscapes, hunky Scots, lots of magic, and happy endings.

She has two ornery fur-babies, plays the piano every day, and loves

Disney and yoga pants more than any twenty-something really should. She is most creative after a good night's sleep and the perfect cup of tea. When not writing, Bethany travels as much as she possibly can, and she never leaves home without a good book to keep her company.

If you want to read more about Bethany or if you're curious about when her next book will come out, please visit her website at: www.bethanyclaire.com, where you can sign up to receive email notifications about new releases.

Made in the USA
San Bernardino, CA
15 April 2018

ACKNOWLEDGMENTS

Without question, I have some of the best team members around.

Karen Corboy, Elizabeth Halliday, Johnetta Ivey, and Vivian Nwankpah, thank you all so much for your willingness to correct, read, and work with our hectic schedule. Your work on these novels is such an integral part of the process. I hope you all know how much I value your input and time.

Dj, thank you for the quick turnaround! You are always so easy to work with, and your edits are vital to the final book.

Mom, I hope you had as much fun on this one as I did. I'm quite certain that we've never had a project that came together so effortlessly from beginning to end. I think we make a wicked good team.